Mills & Boon

BEST SELLER ROMANCE

A chance to read and collect some of the best-loved novels
from Mills & Boon—the world's largest publisher of romantic
fiction.

Every month, three titles by favourite Mills & Boon authors
will be re-published in the *Best Seller Romance* series.

A list of other titles in the *Best Seller Romance* series can be
found at the end of this book.

Carole Mortimer

FEAR OF
LOVE

MILLS & BOON LIMITED
15–16 BROOK'S MEWS
LONDON W1A 1DR

First published in Great Britain 1980
by Mills & Boon Limited

© Carole Mortimer 1980

Australian copyright 1980
Philippine copyright 1980
Reprinted 1980
This edition 1986

ISBN 0 263 75370 0

Set in Linotype Times 10 on 11 pt.
02–0186

Made and printed in Great Britain by
Richard Clay (The Chaucer Press) Ltd,
Bungay, Suffolk

CHAPTER ONE

'Is *he* coming to lunch again?' Alexandra demanded, seeing the four places set at the table.

Gail sighed, despairing of her young sister's manners. 'If you mean Dominic then say so,' she said disapprovingly, moving into the kitchen.

'All right. Is *Dominic* coming to lunch again?'

'Well, as he always comes on a Sunday when he's at home it's a natural assumption to make.' She turned the vegetables down on the cooker. 'Now if you've nothing better to do perhaps you would like to get out the wine glasses. It was your turn to cook lunch today,' she added sternly. 'Where did you disappear to so quickly after breakfast?'

'I met Roger.' Alexandra rubbed the wine glasses to a fine shine before placing them in the appropriate places on the table, a slight smile curving her lips as she thought of the man she loved.

Her sister frowned. 'You seem to do little else lately.'

'Well, if you would let me marry him I wouldn't need to keep going to his parents' house, we could be together all the time.'

'You're too young to get married,' Gail stated emphatically. 'You're seventeen years old and you only left school six months ago. You've only really known Roger four months.'

'Oh, that isn't true! We've lived in this area for years and I've known Roger all of that time.' Alexandra placed the wine in the refrigerator to chill.

'We've lived in this house approximately three years, and two and a half years of that time you were away at

5

boarding-school.' Gail shook her head at her sister's obstinacy, knowing that pouting look of old. But in the case of Alexandra marrying she was adamant. Besides, Roger was only twenty himself. They were both much too young to know their own minds.

'But I've known Roger for simply *ages*!' She had been completely bowled over by his dark rugged good looks as soon as she had seen him at a local dance four months ago, and he appeared to be equally smitten. They had been seeing each other every day since and they were never bored with each other. And Roger's kisses thrilled her like nothing else she had ever known.

Gail gave a light smile. 'I wouldn't call four months ages.' She turned back to the preparation of the meal. 'The men should be arriving soon.'

Alexandra scowled. 'Yes, I suppose Dominic could be called that all right. The typical he-man type,' she sneered, her blue, almost violet eyes flashing her dislike.

'He has a very exciting job,' Gail defended. 'There aren't many men who could take the risks he does.'

'Oh, no, I realise that,' Alexandra said scornfully. 'Travelling around the world filming the latest disaster is life and breath to Dominic. It even meant more to him than his marriage did.'

Now it was Gail's turn to be angry. 'You have no right to judge him. How do you know he didn't take up this sort of life as a means of getting away from his marriage? He and Marianne were never right for each other.'

'You can say that now, now that they're divorced. But they must have been in love once.'

'I'm not saying they weren't, all I am saying is that it wasn't because of the danger of his job that Marianne left him. She was probably too young when they married, which is why he——' Gail broke off, biting her bottom lip.

'Yes?' Alexandra prompted, noting the almost guilty

look on her sister's face. 'Why he what?'

'Nothing. It isn't important.'

'It was important enough for you to clam up.' Her blue eyes narrowed. 'Come on, Gail, I know that look. You're holding something back.'

'Don't be silly. I think I hear a car,' Gail said desperately.

'Never mind that,' Alexandra sighed impatiently. 'Tell me what Dominic did.'

'I told you it wasn't important.'

'It was something to do with me, wasn't it? Something he said, something about my being too young to marry. Was that it, Gail?'

'We did talk it over with him, yes. And he said he didn't think it was a good idea. Now calm down, Alexandra,' Gail pleaded as she saw the angry sparkle in her sister's eyes. 'Trevor and I had already discussed it and come to the same conclusion.'

'But Dominic's disapproval finally convinced you. Don't deny it,' Alexandra commanded fiercely. 'I know how arrogantly autocratic he can be. You probably asked his permission before you went in for this baby you're expecting too. Well, he's gone too far this time, interfered in my life once too often. And I'm going to tell him so!' She marched purposefully to the door.

Gail looked alarmed. 'Where are you going?'

'To see the lordly Dominic Tempest, where else?'

'But he'll probably be here in a moment.'

Alexandra smiled her satisfaction. 'He may be. But in the meantime I mean to go in search of him.'

'You aren't going to cause a scene?' Gail asked wearily, recognising those bright wings of colour in Alexandra's cheeks as the start of her fiery temper.

'*I* didn't cause this scene, Dominic did. He's much too fond of making his opinion known. You may have to take it, Gail, he's your brother-in-law, but he's nothing to me. I've always seen more of him on television than I have around here. I know it's wicked to think it, but I could almost wish for another disaster to happen just so he would leave again.'

'Alexandra!'

'I said it was wicked. But he's been here for four weeks now, quite a record, and he's making me feel claustrophobic. It now seems I have more reason to wish for his departure than I realised. I'll see you later, Gail.'

'But your lunch is ready,' her sister cried.

'Suddenly I'm not hungry,' said Alexandra defiantly.

Trevor was out in the hallway removing his sheepskin jacket. He looked surprised as Alexandra walked straight past him to the front door. 'Hey,' he called. 'Don't hard-working doctors deserve a brotherly kiss any more?'

She hurried back to give him a quick kiss. She did indeed love him as a brother. He had been in her life so long now, he and Gail caring for her since the death of her mother four years ago. Her father had died when she was a very young child and she hardly remembered him, making it easy for Trevor, ten years her senior, to become the steadying male figure in her life. But at the moment she wasn't in the mood to be steadied. Damn Dominic Tempest and his arrogance!

'I'll see you later, Trevor.' She went back to the door.

'But where are you going?' He looked dazed.

'I have to go out for a while. I shouldn't be too long.'

'First Dominic and now you,' he shook his head. 'I only hope Gail can hold lunch back half an hour or so.'

'Dominic has been delayed?' she asked casually.

'Mm, something turned up unexpectedly. He'll be here in about twenty minutes.'

'I'm sure Gail can hold lunch back,' she gave him a bright smile. 'I should be back by then too.'

He shrugged resignedly. 'Okay.'

Alexandra revved up her little Mini before accelerating

away with a screech of tyres. It was a ten-minute drive to the Tempest mansion, which should give her time to get there before Dominic himself left. The mood she was in it shouldn't take her ten minutes, more like five.

Dominic's car was parked in the forecourt of the house ready for his departure, but there was another car there too, not as impressive as the Ferrari, but nevertheless it put her Mini in the shade. It looked like a Lotus Elan.

She didn't have time to confirm this one way or the other because as she got out of her car two people also came out of the house. The man was instantly recognisable as Dominic Tempest, there was no mistaking that powerful physique, the deeply tanned handsome features, and the over-long sun-bleached blond hair. The woman wasn't known to her, but she did look vaguely familiar as she laughed up at the man at her side.

So it wasn't a some*thing* that had come up to delay Dominic, but a some*one*. And she hadn't just arrived, by the look of the overnight case in her hand. Alexandra watched them unobserved for several minutes, watched in disgust as Dominic bent his head to kiss the woman passionately on the lips, and turned away with even more disgust as the woman pressed herself against him for even closer contact. Alexandra found it distasteful of them to make such a public display of their intimate relationship.

As the embrace ended Dominic at last seemed to become aware of Alexandra's presence on the driveway, but he made no attempt to remove the arm of complete possession he had around the woman's shoulders.

He walked towards her with that long easy swagger of his, his grey eyes narrowing at her scornful expression. 'Hello, Alexandra. I'm just on my way, there was no need to send out a search party.' His voice was deep and just as attractive as the rest of him. He was very tall, well over six foot, with carved granite-like features that always seemed to mock or taunt her. He wore his clothes with a lazy elegance that drew attention to him whether he wore denims or a suit. No, she could never deny that he was an attractive man, but at thirty-four he had cashed in on that attraction, having one ex-wife to his credit already, and goodness knows how many mistresses. 'I called Trevor and told him I'd been delayed,' he added.

She nodded. 'Yes, I know. He said *something* had come up.' She gave the woman at his side a cool look.

Dominic's mouth tightened into a thin uncompromising line, the usual sensuousness of that mouth erased by anger. 'Alexandra, I would like you to meet Sabrina Gilbert. Sabrina, Alexandra Paige, my brother's sister-in-law.'

The two women shook hands, Alexandra noting that he gave her no explanation of who Sabrina Gilbert was. Not that she needed to be told, not after the embrace she had witnessed. Besides, Dominic looked as if he had just got out of bed, judging by the look of sleepy satisfaction in his eyes. The whole thing shocked and disgusted her.

'So what are you doing here, Alexandra?' he asked curtly.

'I wanted to talk to you, alone.'

He gave a husky laugh. 'Did it have to be now? I would have been over for lunch in a few minutes. We could have talked then.'

Her mouth set stubbornly. 'I said alone.'

He looked at her sharply. 'I'm sure we have nothing to say to each other that Gail and Trevor can't hear.'

'Not to each other, no. But I have some things to say to you I would prefer no one else to hear.'

'Sounds interesting, darling.' Sabrina Gilbert spoke for the first time, a low husky sound that probably excited men just to hear it. 'I think I'll just be on my way and leave you to it.' She raised her face for his kiss. 'I'll see you at your apartment during the week. Nice to have met you, Miss Paige.'

Alexandra didn't answer, turning away as Dominic lingered over kissing that pouting red mouth. Sabrina was obviously a beautiful woman, with a bright cap of golden hair, come-to-bed blue eyes, and a perfect figure, but Alexandra didn't think that Dominic had to make quite such a meal of her.

'I'll call you Tuesday or Wednesday,' he promised throatily.

'I'll be waiting.' She got into the Lotus Elan and with a wave of her hand drove off.

Dominic turned his icy grey eyes on Alexandra, his anger a tangible thing. 'Now perhaps we can have that talk you seem to want,' he said in a clipped voice.

Her blue eyes flashed her dislike of him. 'I think you're the lowest, most contemptible——'

He grasped her arm, dragging her towards the house. 'Not out here,' he growled. 'Have the good manners to wait until we're in my study. That is, of course, if you know what good manners are. You haven't given a very good impression of it so far.'

'What did you expect me to do while you drooled over the lovely Miss Gilbert?' she sneered. 'Stand and clap your performance?'

He looked down at her. 'If you felt it merited it.' He pushed her into a room. 'But I was referring to your behaviour before then.' He leant back against his desk, his arms folded challengingly in front of his chest. 'That was the most disgusting display of bad manners you've shown in a long time.'

Her eyes blazed. 'How dare you! I——'

He gave a humourless smile. 'How dare *I*?' He shook his head. 'I haven't done anything, Alex. You stormed over here——'

'Don't call me Alex!' she snapped. 'It makes me sound

like a boy. My name is Alexandra.'

Those grey eyes travelled slowly over her taut angry body clothed in denims and a tee-shirt. 'Well, you dress like a boy, but the shape is definitely female. I hadn't realised quite how much you've grown up.'

His gaze was positively insolent and Alexandra only just stopped herself putting up shielding hands to cover her body. Thank goodness she did, she could just imagine the mockery he would show her if she had given in to such a weakness. But he had no right to look at her that way when he had just got out of bed with the sexy blonde. He had no right to look at her like that anyway, almost as if he were mentally undressing her.

She found herself blushing anyway, unable to stop the involuntary action. This was the first time Dominic had shown in any way that he regarded her as a woman. It was vaguely unnerving and she felt tongue-tied.

But of course he was looking at her as a woman, his senses were probably still aflame from the weekend spent with the lovely Sabrina Gilbert. Alexandra now realised where she had seen the other woman; she appeared in a popular long-running television series. The two of them had probably met at the television studio where Dominic recorded his weekly current affairs programme.

'It's because I'm grown up that I'm here,' she said finally, her cheeks still aflame.

'Really?' he drawled. 'Have you come over for some private tuition?'

Her mouth tightened. 'Don't be ridiculous! If I required that sort of tuition I certainly wouldn't come to you for it. I have a boy-friend who can supply me with all the experience I need.'

Those grey eyes narrowed. 'Roger Young.' His top lip curled back contmptuously.

'Yes! And he's the reason I've come over here.'

'He is? Well, I'm not about to give him any tuition,'

he taunted. 'It wouldn't be half as much fun.'

'Ooh, you're such a conceited swine!' Alexandra stamped her foot in childish temper. 'Just because you've slept with more women than you can remember the names of you think you know it all! I happen to believe that making love is more than just sex between two people, it should be something private between man and wife.'

The contempt was still there in his face and it was directed at her now. 'I've tried being married. Believe me, it isn't all it's supposed to be.'

'You were married for exactly a year, hardly long enough to be able to pass comment on it. You treated your wife shamefully.'

'Did I now?' he mused. 'And what would you know about it? You would have been five at the time, and as we didn't even know you then I don't consider you in a position to judge how I treated my wife.'

'I didn't need to know you when you were married to know it was all your fault that the marriage failed. I know for a fact that you weren't even in the same country six months out of the twelve.'

Dominic looked angry now. 'Like I said, you aren't in a position to judge.'

'I am when it affects my life,' she told him crossly.

'What does my marriage have to do with your life?'

'Gail told me this morning that it was mainly due to your disapproval of the idea that they refused to give their consent to my marriage to Roger.'

'I see,' he nodded his head, his look thoughtful. 'Gail told you that, did she?'

She flushed. 'With a little persuasion, yes.'

Dominic's mouth twisted. 'I can imagine what type of persuasion. You're a bully, Alexandra. And you're spoilt too. Poor Gail doesn't stand a chance when you have one of your tantrums.'

'I do not have tantrums!'

'Oh yes, you do, and Gail isn't strong enough to say no to you, neither is Trevor for that matter. You're wilful and utterly selfish and not grown up enough to marry anyone, let alone a kid like Roger Young. He's just as spoilt as you are.'

'You have a nerve!' she exclaimed furiously.

'Not really,' he answered calmly. 'I just thought it better to stop you becoming just another statistic in the divorce figures.'

'And you're arrogant too,' she continued. 'You have no way of knowing whether my marriage to Roger will succeed or not.'

'I can take a pretty accurate guess,' he drawled. 'I'll also make another guess, that by the time you reach your eighteenth birthday in a few months' time you'll have changed your mind about marrying him.'

'I will not,' she said indignantly. 'I love him.'

He smiled at her outburst. 'You say you do now, I wonder if you'll feel the same in six months' time. I doubt it. You're at an age when you fall in and out of love every month.'

'Like your wife did?' she taunted bitterly.

'Exactly as Marianne did,' he agreed tautly.

Alerandra realised that perhaps she had gone too far this time. 'I'm sorry,' she said, shamefaced. 'I shouldn't have said that.'

'Oh, don't start apologising now, Alexandra. We've gone way past the stage of not being able to speak our minds to each other.'

'Yes, I suppose so.'

He smiled. 'I know so. Look, Alex—Alexandra,' he amended. 'I'm older than you, exactly twice your age, and I can see the pitfalls of marrying at your age. Marianne was no older than you when we married, and look how disastrously that turned out. We were divorced before she reached nineteen.'

'You can't compare me with her—or my intended husband with you.'

'Meaning?'

She didn't flinch from his icy grey eyes. 'Meaning that there is no way Roger can be compared with you. He doesn't have to keep proving his sexual prowess, whereas you—well, it's pretty obvious that your *guest* didn't sleep in any other bedroom but your own. Is she your latest mistress?'

Dominic raised his eyebrows. 'What does that have to do with you?'

She shrugged. 'I was just curious.' She flicked back her long black hair, long sooty lashes surrounding her deep blue eyes. 'Is she?'

'Yes,' he answered with violence.

'But you don't intend marrying her?' Alexandra's curiosity had got the better of her now.

'I don't intend marrying ever again.'

'Does she know that?'

'Oh yes,' he smiled. 'Sabrina knows exactly what I feel for her.'

'I'll bet she does,' her mouth turned back with distaste. 'But I still maintain that you had no right to interfere in my life. I love Roger and I want to marry him.'

'I didn't stop you. I merely told Gail and Trevor that I——'

'Didn't think it a good idea,' she snapped. 'It was nothing to do with you, nothing at all.'

'I'm sure that what I said meant little to either of them, they'd already made up their minds about it.'

She shook her head. 'I don't agree. I think what you had to say had everything to do with their decision. They hardly dare breathe without your permission. I'm well aware of the fact that you've helped them out a lot since they married, but I don't want to be included in that care.

I want you to just stay out of my life.'

'A little late for that, isn't it?'

She looked at him sharply. 'What do you mean?'

He shrugged. 'It isn't important. Let's just accept that I'm the villain of the piece and forget it.'

Alexandra's mouth set angrily. 'I don't want to forget it. I want to know what you meant just now. What else have you had a hand in that I know nothing about?'

'I said it isn't important.' He looked at his wrist-watch. 'I have to leave now, I'm much later than the twenty minutes I said I would be.'

'Dominic,' she held his arm. 'Please tell me.' Her look was pleading.

He looked down pointedly at her hand on his tanned forearm and she snatched it away hurriedly. 'There's nothing to tell. Let's go,' he pulled her out of the house. 'We can talk some other time.'

She wrenched out of his grasp. 'We'll talk now! I——'

Charles, the butler, appeared in the open doorway. 'Telephone for you, sir. It's Mr Trevor,' he added.

'Tell him I'm on my way, Charles,' Dominic answered him.

'I did that, sir. But he says he has to speak to you urgently.'

'Very well, Charles. Tell him I'll be right there.'

'Yes, sir.' The butler disappeared back into the house.

Dominic gave Alexandra an impatient look. 'Wait here and we can drive back together.'

'Forget it.' She ran down the remaining steps to the driveway. 'I've seen you quite enough for one day.'

'Alexandra, you'll wait——'

'Goodbye, Dominic.' She walked hurriedly away as he turned angrily to go and answer the telephone.

There were still quite a lot of questions she would like answers to, but she was just too angry to talk to him any more. She would go straight over and see Roger, he always put her in a better mood.

As she accelerated the Mini past the house Dominic rushed out of the doorway, waving frantically for her to stop. She gave him an impudent grin and cheekily waved back. She smiled as she looked in the driving mirror as she saw him standing in the driveway angrily watching her leave.

Just thwarting him in this way put her in a better humour and by the time she reached Roger's parents' house she was feeling much happier. They should have finished lunch, it was after two o'clock, so she felt no hesitation about knocking on the door.

She was shown into the lounge where the Young family were just having their coffee. Her eyes went instantly to Roger, her heart pounding loudly just at the sight of him. He looked pleased to see her too and they smiled dreamily at each other.

'Hello, my dear,' Mrs Young greeted politely. 'Would you like to join us in some coffee?'

The rumblings of her stomach told her that she should really have gone home and had her lunch before coming here, but as she hadn't the coffee would have to sustain her until her evening meal. 'Yes, please, Mrs Young.'

Roger made room for her on the sofa beside him, his arm about her shoulders pulling her close against his side. 'You're over early today,' he murmured softly.

She snuggled against him. 'Does that mean you aren't pleased to see me?'

His hold tightened. 'Don't say that! I just wasn't expecting you yet.'

Alexandra sat up as his mother handed her the cup of steaming coffee. 'Thank you,' she smiled.

Roger was frowning. 'I don't see how you can possibly have eaten lunch and got over here since we parted at the pool this morning.'

She squeezed his hand reassuringly. 'I'll explain later.'

'Yes, but——'

'How is your sister keeping?' Mrs Young asked her. 'I should think she's getting quite impatient now.'

'A little,' Alexandra agreed. 'Only another four weeks to go.'

'I suppose that brother-in-law of yours is kept busy at the hospital,' put in Mr Young. 'Although it must be quite convenient having a doctor in the house.'

'Yes,' she smiled. She liked Roger's parents immensely, although they tended to be a little possessive about their only child. Both in their mid-fifties, they had had Roger after ten years of marriage, and he was destined to be the only child they would have. After his initial training he was expected to join his father's law firm.

The Youngs were the nearest thing the village had to the local people of the manor, the large house they owned set in vast woodlands. With Mrs Young's twin-sets and tweed skirts and Mr Young riding to hounds and arranging shooting parties, they were everything that could be expected of real gentry.

'Would you like a game of tennis?' Roger asked her softly, the gleam in his deep brown eyes showing that he had more than tennis in mind.

'Let the girl finish her coffee,' his father said sternly.

'But I have.' Alexandra put her empty cup down in the tray.

'You can't go running about a tennis court now, Roger,' his mother reprimanded. 'You've only just eaten.'

'We'll be fine,' he pulled Alexandra to her feet. 'See you later.'

Alexandra giggled once they were outside. 'Don't you ever listen to your parents?'

He grinned. 'Not usually. They tend to fuss too much.'

'They love you, that's why.'

He took her hand in his own, leading her round to the garden at the back of the house, the green lawns stretching down to the tennis courts just out of sight of the house. 'They still fuss too much.' He pulled her close against him, his lips lingering on hers. 'I've missed you,' he said throatily.

She blushed. 'We only parted two hours ago.'

'Much too long.' He kissed her again. 'Now tell me why you haven't eaten lunch?'

She stood back. 'How did you know that?'

'You haven't had time. Did something happen?'

'Let's go down to the tennis court, we can talk better there.'

'Something *did* happen,' he said.

She laughed. 'Come on, it's nothing we can't sort out.'

They walked down to the comparative privacy of the tennis courts, sitting down on the seats provided, tennis the last thing on their minds at the moment. Their kiss lasted for a long time, and both of them were breathless at the end of it.

'Mm,' Roger's face was buried in her throat. 'I wish we were married.'

It reminded her too much of her scene with Dominic Tempest earlier and she moved out of Roger's arms, an angry glitter to her big blue eyes. 'It's funny you should mention that. I found out the reason for Gail and Trevor's refusal today. Trevor's bossy brother put his spoke in.'

Roger frowned. 'Dominic Tempest did?'

She grimaced. 'The same.'

'But I don't see what it has to do with him.'

'Neither did I, and I told him so. I think he's got the message now.'

'Mm, well as long as he has.'

'He has,' she said with certainty.

'And he's the reason you haven't eaten?'

'I could hardly sit down to lunch with him after the things I'd just said,' she smiled at the memory. 'I wasn't very polite.'

'You never are when you speak to him. I've only ever met him twice, at your sister's house, and each time you argued with him.'

'Only because he has such strong views on everything. He always thinks he's right.'

Roger chuckled. 'So do you.'

'Maybe, but I'm certainly not going to agree with everything he says like Gail and Trevor do. It makes me sick the way they always do what he says. Just because he appears on the television it doesn't make him anything special.'

'His programmes are very interesting,' Roger pointed out.

'So they ought to be, the risks he takes. I'm surprised he hasn't killed himself by now.'

'Someone has to take those risks or we would never know what was going on in the world,' he pointed out reasonably.

'I know that, but does he have to enjoy it so much?'

'A man should enjoy his work, he's going to be doing it for years.'

'Not that sort of job he isn't. He'll be too old for it soon. He's thirty-four, you know.'

Roger chuckled. 'That isn't old. Will you think me old and past it when I get to that age?'

'Oh, he isn't past it, far from it. He had some woman staying with him this weekend, and he openly admitted to sleeping with her.'

'Goodness, your conversation did get personal, didn't it?' grinned Roger.

'Very. Oh, let's forget about him, he only angers me.'

'I'm all for that,' he said throatily. 'Kiss me some more.'

She did, her arms about his neck, her body pressed against him. They were so engrossed in each other they didn't hear the approaching footsteps on the gravel pathway.

'I hate to interrupt the two of you,' drawled a familiar taunting voice, 'but I have to take you home, Alexandra.'

She looked up at Dominic Tempest, her hair wild, her eyes slightly glazed and her mouth bare of lipstick. She moved hurriedly out of Roger's arms, smoothing her hair down self-consciously.

She licked her lips. 'What did you say? And what are you doing here anyway?' she asked resentfully, some of her composure returning. Why should she feel embarassed? He hadn't this morning.

'I've come to take you home,' he repeated. 'Roger's parents told me you were down here.'

Alexandra stood up, challenge in every line of her body. 'What do you mean, you've come to take me home? Just who do you think you are? I don't have——'

'Gail's been taken to hospital, Alex,' Dominic told her quietly.

Her face paled. 'To hospital? But why? I don't understand.'

'It's quite simple. She collapsed shortly after you walked out of there this morning,' he told her calmly.

'Oh, darling!' Roger held her in his arms, kissing her forehead gently. 'She'll be all right, Alexandra, I'm sure of it.'

'Oh yes, she'll be all right,' Dominic Tempest agreed coldly. 'Now that she's safely in hospital away from Alexandra's childish displays of temper.'

CHAPTER TWO

ROGER flushed furiously. 'Now look here, you can't go around saying things like that! Alexandra can't be held responsible for——'

'I think Alex knows she can be held entirely responsible,' the elder man interrupted. 'She knew the delicacy of Gail's condition, but she went ahead with her stupid personal grudge against me, walking out of the house swearing vengeance for some wrong she believes me to have done her.'

'But you——'

'He's right, Roger,' Alexandra said dully. 'I did walk out of the house with the intention of going to see him, and I did tell Gail. She's eight months pregnant, I should have realised it would upset her.'

'Yes, you should have,' Dominic agreed abruptly. 'Like I told you earlier, you're utterly selfish. Now, if you're ready, I'll take you to the hospital. Gail will want to see you.'

'Is she going to be all right?' Her eyes pleaded for him to say yes.

'With rest and being kept under observation they think she's going to be fine, no thanks to you.'

'That's enough, Tempest,' Roger said angrily. 'Can't you see how upset she is? There's no need to keep saying things like that to her.'

'There's every need, damn you!' Dominic snapped forcefully. 'Alexandra has to be made to see how her thoughtlessness can hurt other people. We're lucky the baby isn't being born right now.'

Alexandra raised distressed eyes. 'It isn't, is it?'

'No,' he gave her an impatient look. 'Are you ready to leave, because I'm going back to the hospital now whether you come or not. Trevor needs a little moral support at the moment.' He turned sharply on his heel and began walking back towards the house.

'Dominic!' she cried out his name, beginning to run after him. 'Wait for me!'

He didn't look at her as she ran to keep up with him. 'I don't have the time.'

She clutched at his arm. 'Please, Dominic,' she pleaded. 'Tell me how Gail is.'

At last he looked at her, his eyes cold. 'I'll tell you in the car if you really want to know, but I've wasted enough time on you for one day. I've been looking for you for over an hour now. Why the hell didn't you stop when I waved you down?'

'I——'

'You thought you were being clever, getting one up on me,' he guessed correctly.

'Well, I—— Was that what the telephone call was about?'

'Yes.' They had reached his car by now. He wrenched open his car door and got in behind the wheel. 'If you want to know any more get in.'

'But—— My car,' she said desperately.

Dominic started the engine. 'Leave it.'

'I can't do that. It——'

'Then don't.' He started to reverse the car out of the driveway.

'Dominic, wait!' She turned desperately to Roger. 'I want to go with him, he can tell me more about Gail on the way. My car—would you drive it over later for me?'

'Of course, darling,' he kissed her lightly on the lips. 'Call me and let me know how your sister is.'

'I will.'

Dominic hardly gave her time to get in the car before

accelerating down the road. 'That kid's like a lapdog,' he remarked grimly. 'He does exactly as you say.'

She flushed angrily. 'He was only trying to be helpful.'

'I hope I didn't interrupt anything just now,' he taunted. 'You looked like you were just getting started.'

'We weren't,' she answered tautly.

He shrugged. 'You looked as if you were. His parents said you were playing tennis, but you looked as if you were playing something else to me.'

'We were just going to play tennis,' she said resentfully.

'It looked like it. And you said my display this morning was disgusting!'

Her eyes flashed her dislike of him. 'I didn't come with you to be insulted. You said you'd tell me about Gail.'

'So far there isn't a lot to tell you, except that she has to stay in hospital.'

She nodded. 'Just for a few days. I can spend the time getting the house spring-cleaned for her return,' she continued eagerly.

Dominic shook his head. 'She isn't staying in for a couple of days, Alex. The doctors have decided it will be better for both her and the baby if she spends the last few weeks before the baby is born resting in a hospital bed.'

'But that—that's four weeks away,' she gasped in dismay. 'She has to stay in all that time?'

'At the moment they think it best.'

'How awful for her! I would hate to be in hospital all that time.'

'So will she, so you can damn well behave yourself when you see her. Gail is to have no worries whatsoever.'

'I wouldn't dream of worrying her,' she said indignantly.

He drove into the car park of the hospital. 'Then make sure you don't.'

'Now look, I don't have to take this from you. You aren't——'

Dominic turned with barely concealed violence to face her. 'You'll take from me exactly what I care to give out! At the moment I could quite easily beat the hell out of you and not feel a moment's remorse.'

Alexandra flung open the door, quickly scrambling out. 'I don't have to stay here and suffer your insults!' She slammed the door.

He was beside her in seconds, swinging her round to face him. 'You'll listen to me for as long as I want you to,' his grey eyes glittered down at her. 'No matter what Gail says to you when you see her you're to agree to it, do you understand?'

She frowned, shaking off his restraining hand. 'No, I don't understand at all. What could Gail possibly say to me that I'm not going to agree with?'

'You'll see. And I want you to know that I'm no happier about the arrangement than you will be.'

'What is it?' she asked suspiciously.

'Wait and see. Come on, let's find Trevor.'

They found him in Gail's hospital room, sitting on the side of the bed holding his wife's hand. Alexandra rushed straight to her sister, the ready tears falling unheeded down her cheeks.

'Oh, Gail,' she sobbed, 'I'm sorry, so sorry.'

Gail cradled her in her arms, laughing softly. 'What on earth are you saying sorry for? It's my own fault I'm here.'

'I——It is?' she looked uncertain.

Gail pushed her young sister's hair away from her tear-wet face. 'Of course, silly. I knew my blood pressure was a little high, I should have slowed down.'

'You mean I should have helped you more. I didn't realise you were ill.'

'I'm not ill, pet,' Gail insisted. 'And you do far too

much at home already. Besides, I enjoy looking after the two of you.'

'Well, now you have to pay for your obstinacy,' Trevor put in lightly.

'And you'll have to sleep alone,' his wife teased. 'You'll have no one to warm your cold feet on now.'

He grimaced. 'The bachelor quarters here aren't very glamorous. But at least I'll be able to visit you when I'm off duty.'

Alexandra frowned. Somewhere along the line she had lost the meaning of this conversation.

'Is it all right for you to move in?' Gail asked Trevor worriedly. 'Have they got a room?'

Her husband squeezed her hand. 'Everything is arranged. I just have to go home and collect a few things.'

Gail looked at her sister. 'You'll be all right at Dominic's, won't you, Alexandra?'

So that was it! She turned to look accusingly at Dominic Tempest and met only his icy disdain. He had known all along that it had been arranged for her to stay at his home with him. How on earth was she going to stand it? One look at Gail's pale face told her that somehow she would have to, Gail simply wasn't up to any more worries.

'Of course I will,' she assured her sister hurriedly. 'I'm sure he'll—he'll take good care of me.'

Dominic moved forward, the mockery in his eyes taunting her. 'You know I will,' he drawled. 'You saw how I like to keep my guests entertained this morning.'

Alexandra raised startled eyes. Yes, she had seen all too clearly how he had entertained his guest over the weekend, and she had no intention of being entertained in the same way. Arrogant devil!

Gail looked interested. 'You had someone staying with you this weekend?'

'Just overnight.' He met Alexandra's scathing look with an unflinching stare.

Trevor stood up. 'I think it's time we left you to get this rest you're supposed to be having.'

His wife pouted. 'I'm sure it isn't necessary. I shall be very lonely in here all on my own.'

'Of course you won't,' Alexandra chided. 'I shall visit you every day, and I'm sure you'll have plenty of other visitors.'

'Not least of all me.' Trevor bent down and kissed his wife lingeringly on the lips. 'I'll be in to see you later.'

Dominic kissed Gail's cheek. 'I'll bring Alexandra in tomorrow,' he promised.

So already he had started to arrange her life for her! She buried her resentment for when they got outside, for the moment intent only on making sure Gail had nothing at all to worry about.

'Look after yourself,' she told her. 'And as Dominic says, I'll be in tomorrow.' Not that *he* would be bringing her, she wanted as little to do with him as possible.

They parted from Trevor once they were outside the room, he having to go back on duty for a few hours before going home to collect his things.

Alexandra waited until they were in Dominic Tempest's car before she exploded. 'You knew about this,' she accused angrily. 'You knew I had to stay with you!'

He raised his eyebrows. 'Your remorse didn't last long.'

She blushed. 'Gail doesn't seem to blame me.'

He shrugged. 'She wouldn't.'

'But you do.'

'It's not up to me to blame you.'

'Then mind your own business! I'm not going to stay at your house, you know,' she told him stubbornly.

'Oh yes, you are,' he said calmly.

'I'm not. I can look after myself. I'm not afraid to stay

at the house on my own.'

'It isn't because we thought you would be afraid that we made these arrangements.'

'Then why? Why does Trevor have to move into the hospital? I'm perfectly capable of looking after him.'

'I don't doubt it,' he said dryly.

'So why all these elaborate plans?'

Dominic sighed. 'They aren't elaborate. They're the most reasonable course of action.'

'Not to me they aren't,' she declared stubbornly.

'No, they wouldn't be. It wouldn't occur to you to think of the damage you could do to Trevor's career and his marriage to Gail by staying at the house with him.'

'What on earth are you talking about?' she scorned. 'Trevor is my brother-in-law.'

'You little fool, do you think that would matter to the people around here? Don't be stupid. All that would matter to them would be that Gail, eight months pregnant, has been taken to hospital, and her husband and young sister are living alone together. This is a village community, Alex, things get around.'

'But surely they wouldn't——' But she knew they would! 'How disgusting!'

'Yes, isn't it?'

'But I don't see how I can be thought any safer living with you. We all know your reputation,' she added bitchily.

Dominic smiled, a cruel mocking smile. 'But I have servants to chaperone us. And for what it's worth, I've never found rebellious adolescents in the least attractive.'

'I hate you!' she said with feeling.

'I couldn't give a damn what you feel for me, I'm not that keen on you either. But I do intend to try and put up with you for the next few weeks, and I hope you will make a similar effort.'

'Why should I? I can live at the house on my own, Gail doesn't need to know.'

'But she would.'

'Why?' she asked sharply. 'Would you tell her? I'm sure you can't be any more anxious to have me at your house than I am to stay there.'

'I'm not,' he agreed coldly. 'But other people in the village are sure to visit Gail and it would only take one thoughtless person to mention where you're living to put her in a state of nerves.'

'But I could——'

'For God's sake grow up, Alexandra!' he snapped. 'Stop thinking of yourself so much. Gail can't take any more, don't you understand?'

She looked down at her hands folded in her lap. 'I suppose so.'

'I'm not at home a lot of the time anyway,' he added by way of consolation. 'I'm away all day Wednesday and Thursday recording the programme.'

'Overnight too?'

His mouth tightened. 'Yes.'

'So that's when you intend seeing Miss Gilbert.'

'Yes.'

'I bet you've got a harem going,' she taunted.

'One woman at a time is enough for me. Besides, I don't have the time for all these women. Each programme I do involves a lot of research, research that has to be done in a matter of hours, not days, if a political situation arises.'

'You haven't been away for some time,' she remarked softly.

He grinned. 'Then you'll just have to hope something comes up during the next four weeks to take me away. I'm sure nothing would please you more.'

'It wouldn't.'

He was openly laughing at her now. 'Sometimes you're an enigma, but in your dislike of me I can see right through you.'

'Good,' she said childishly.

'Oh, by the way,' he remarked casually, 'I don't mind you having Young round occasionally, but I don't want to keep tripping over him.'

Alexandra glared at him. 'Am I allowed to make the same comment about Miss Gilbert?'

'No.'

'I didn't think I would be.'

Dominic gave her an impatient look. 'You aren't a welcome guest, Alexandra, so I don't intend letting your friends take over my house.'

'I take it Miss Gilbert is a welcome guest?'

'You take it right.'

'Don't worry, Dominic,' she said sharply. 'If I want to see any of my friends I'll arrange to meet them elsewhere than your house.'

'There's no need to go to that extreme,' he taunted.

Alexandra looked out of the car window as they approached the mansion that was to be her home for the next month. How on earth could she stand to share a house with this arrogant mocking man, see him every day for four weeks, when she found it difficult to be polite to him just during Sunday lunch? It appeared she had little choice but to try.

Charles met them in the reception area. 'I have prepared Miss Paige's room, sir.'

His employer nodded, and threw his car keys down on the side-table. 'Thank you, Charles. Perhaps you would like to freshen up before tea, Alexandra?'

She didn't think this was going to be the normal cup of tea and a biscuit she and Gail usually shared in the afternoon, and her denims and tee shirt suddenly seemed out of place in these elegant surroundings.

'Thank you,' she accepted softly, 'I'd like that.'

'I'll take you upstairs now,' Charles said gravely.

It was a lovely room he showed her into, all lemon and white decor. It had its own adjoining bathroom, a luxury she had never had before. She and Trevor usually fought over who would get into the bathroom first in the morning.

The adjoining bathroom was in lemon and brown, but she didn't stay to admire it, quickly rinsing her face and hands before brushing her hair and applying a lip-gloss. The rumblings of her stomach were far too strong for her to waste any more time. She hadn't eaten anything since breakfast this morning and she was starving hungry.

Dominic was sitting in the lounge when she came hesitantly into the room, stubbing his cheroot out in the ashtray at her entrance. His elegant light grey trousers and black fitted shirt only seemed to emphasise her own scruffiness. Well, how was she supposed to know she would be taking tea with the famous Dominic Tempest!

'Sit down, Alexandra,' he said impatiently. 'You might as well play hostess.'

She blushed at his scathing mockery. 'I'd rather not.'

'Oh, come on, Alex,' he encouraged shortly. 'I'm as hungry as you are. I missed out on lunch too, remember?'

She picked up the china teapot. 'I didn't know you admitted to such human feelings as hunger.'

His grey eyes taunted. 'I admit to much more human feelings than that.'

She should have known her effort to hit out at him would only rebound on her. 'Lemon, milk and sugar?' she asked tightly.

'Just lemon, please. I'm sweet enough already.'

'That's a matter of opinion!'

He laughed, showing even white teeth in his tanned face. 'Somehow I knew you would say that.'

'Then I'm glad you weren't disappointed.'

He took the proffered cup of tea. 'You never disappoint me, Alex. You're very entertaining.'

She poured her own tea. 'I'm glad I'm of some use!'

He raised his eyebrows. 'Oh dear, is it feel sorry for Alex day?'

Her blue eyes showed her anger. 'No, it isn't! And my name is Alexandra.'

'So it is,' he appeared unconcerned. 'But I prefer Alex. Much more friendly.'

'As I have no intention of becoming a friend of yours I would prefer you to use my full name.'

'And I would prefer not to. Oh, shut up, Alex,' he ordered abruptly as she went to speak again. 'And pass me a sandwich.'

Her cup landed with a clatter on the table. 'I may have to stay here with you, but I'm certainly not going to be reduced to the level of another servant for you to order about!'

'If you were a servant we might get on better,' he retorted. 'I happen to like all my employees. But I would certainly never take from them what I've taken from you today.'

'Don't expect the next month to be any different.' She bit hungrily into a ham sandwich. 'Staying here won't make me like you any the more.'

Dominic raised his eyes heavenwards, pushing the blond hair back off his forehead. 'Thank God you'll be out of the house most of the time.'

'I will?'

'I hope so. College should—oh no!' he groaned. 'College has finished for the summer, hasn't it?'

She smiled sweetly. 'It has.'

'Oh hell!'

'Temper, temper,' she taunted. 'Anyone would think you weren't going to enjoy having me about.'

'Anyone would be right,' he said dryly.

'Shame!' Alexandra laughed. 'Could I use your telephone, please?'

'I'm surprised you bothered to ask.'

Alexandra ignored his mockery. 'Well, can I?'

'I suppose you're going to call lover boy?'

Her head rose haughtily. 'If you mean Roger, then yes, I am.'

Dominic looked bored. 'Go ahead. But remember what I said about inviting him round here. I'm not as liberal as Gail and Trevor, I won't allow you to take him upstairs to your bedroom. I'm too much aware of the temptation involved.'

'You would be. Roger and I don't regard it in that light. We merely go to my room to listen to records.'

'More fool you.' He stood up. 'I'm going to my study, so you can use the telephone in here. I would appreciate it if you didn't disturb me, I have some work to do.'

'I have no intention of disturbing you,' she said indignantly.

'Fine. When you've finished with the tea things just ring for Charles and he'll clear away. Dinner is at eight, by the way.'

'Am I expected to dress up for that?'

'Not particularly.' His eyes travelled slowly over her slender body. 'But I think I would prefer you to put on something more feminine than denims.'

'Your likes and dislikes don't come into it,' she told him sharply. 'But I have to go back to the house and pack a few things, so I might manage to change for dinner.'

'You're going to the house now?'

She gave him a challenging look. 'Do you have any objections?'

'None, as long as you don't use it as a meeting place for yourself and your boy-friend.'

'You have a disgusting mind, Mr Tempest!'

He laughed at her outrage. 'I'm just realistic, *Alex.*'

She was still glowering at him as he left the room

She couldn't stay here with him, she just couldn't. They didn't even like each other. But she didn't see what else she could do; Gail's health depended on her not causing trouble.

She put a call through to the hospital before calling Roger, and was told that Mrs Tempest was asleep and not to be disturbed. It seemed to underline the fact that Gail's health was very delicate at the moment. She left a message for them to tell Gail of her call and she sent her love.

Her call to Roger wasn't quite so easy, knowing he wouldn't understand her reasons for being at Dominic Tempest's house any better than she did herself. She was right, he didn't.

'You could come and stay here,' he suggested. 'My mother and father would love to have you.'

'I—I never thought of that.' Hope quickened her heart. 'Do you really think they wouldn't mind?'

'I know they wouldn't.'

'Wait a minute, then, and I'll go and see what Dominic says,' she said eagerly.

'What does it matter what he says?' Roger demanded crossly. 'After the way he spoke to you earlier I can't believe it would bother him where you stay.'

'You're right, it doesn't. But I— Look, I'll just see what he thinks of the idea.' She put the telephone down before he could raise any more objections. She knocked briskly on Dominic's study door before entering.

He looked up at her, an impatient frown marking his forehead. 'I thought I said I wasn't to be disturbed,' he snapped coldly. 'God, you've only been in the house an hour and already you're making a nuisance of yourself.'

Angry colour flared into her cheeks. 'I did knock!'

Dominic sat back, his eyes narrowed. 'So I heard, but I don't remember inviting you in.'

'You're impossible!'

'Instead of standing there getting angry I think you would be better spending the time telling me what you came in here for, because in two minutes you're going to be thrown out again.'

'It doesn't matter!' She turned on her heel.

'Alexandra!' her name sounded like a whiplash. 'Get back in here.'

She blinked back the tears. 'No, I won't.'

Dominic sighed. 'You came to ask me something, you might as well do that now you're here.'

'I said it doesn't matter,' she said obstinately.

'You have one minute left,' he warned.

Alexandra turned angrily. 'Is your time so valuable you don't have two minutes to spare?'

'At the moment, yes. I have a schedule to meet. So what's wrong?'

'Roger's on the telephone, he says I can stay at his house.'

'No.'

Her eyes were a deeper blue as her anger increased. 'What do you mean, no? Why can't I? Who's to say I can't anyway?'

'I am,' he told her calmly. 'In view of the absence of Gail and Trevor I'm acting as your guardian, and I say you stay where you are. Now, if that's all you wanted I have work to do.'

'You have no right——'

'I have every right! You're staying here, where Gail and Trevor can be sure you're safe.'

'With you?' she scorned.

'With me,' he said grimly.

'You're just being pigheaded about this,' she said angrily. 'I've stayed at Roger's house several weekends in the past. Gail and Trevor didn't mind at all.'

'A weekend is completely different from a full month. It could be even longer, we have no guarantee when

Gail's going to have the baby. No, you go back and tell your boy-friend that you're staying here.'

She slammed the door behind her. He was nothing but a bully and a tyrant! She snatched up the telephone receiver. 'Mr Tempest doesn't think it's a good idea,' she snapped.

'Damn him, he doesn't have any say in it!' Roger sounded as angry as she was herself.

'He thinks he does.' She sighed, relaxing her body somewhat. 'Can you come and pick me up, I have to go and collect some of my clothes? I'll wait for you outside, I find this place oppressive.'

They arranged to meet in half an hour, and for Alexandra the time dragged by. She ran over to the car when Roger arrived, getting in beside him before he had hardly had time to stop.

She leant over and kissed him hurriedly on the lips. 'Let's get out of here.'

Roger looked at her closely. 'Hey, Alexandra, I'm sure that if you explained to your sister or Trevor how much you dislike being at Tempest's house they wouldn't expect you to stay.'

'Gail isn't to be worried and Trevor already has enough to think about. I don't want to talk about it any more, Roger.'

'Yes, but——'

'Forget it,' she said fiercely.

'But if it's upsetting you, Alexandra,' he persisted.

She smiled. 'There are worse things in life than living in luxury at Dominic Tempest's for the next four weeks.' But she couldn't for the life of her think of one right now!

She let them into the house with her key, exclaiming her dismay at the chaos in the kitchen. She had forgotten they were about to have lunch when Gail's collapse had occurred. She set Roger to washing up while she defrosted the refrigerator.

Everything cleared away, she went up to her room to pack her suitcase. Roger stood in the doorway watching her.

'So he's graciously permitted me to call occasionally,' he said sarcastically.

'Who?' She unlocked her wardrobe. 'Oh, *him*! Yes,' she sorted through her clothing. 'As long as we don't bother him.'

'The less I have to do with him the better.'

'That's what I told him.' She sat down on the bed with a laugh. 'I feel almost sorry for him. This time yesterday he was basking in the loving attention of his mistress, and now he has me foisted on him.' She began to laugh in earnest now. 'And I'm not exactly the easiest of people to suddenly have in your life.'

Roger came to sit next to her. 'I like having you in my life,' he said throatily.

She smiled at him. 'It isn't exactly the same thing. To Dominic I'm just a nuisance, he said so this afternoon.'

He put his arm about her shoulders, kissing her softly on the lips. 'I don't give a damn what he says, I think you're lovely.' He pulled her closer, the pressure of his lips increasing.

'Oh, Roger,' she breathed against his mouth.

'Mm,' he kissed her again. 'I love you.'

'I love you too.'

He pushed her back against the pillows, his lips travelling slowly over her throat and back to her mouth. They were slow drugging kisses and she felt herself responding to them without reserve.

She began to feel her first feelings of restraint when his hands began to roam beneath her tee-shirt, and she pulled back from him. 'What are you doing?' Her panic was obvious.

He was trembling against her. 'I love you, Alexandra.

And I—I want you.'

'Roger!' She was shocked now. 'You can't—*we* can't.'

'Of course we can,' he kissed her again. 'We're going to be married soon.'

Alexandra pushed against him. 'That isn't the point Roger. We aren't married now.'

'Don't be such a prude!' He held her roughly. 'We're all alone here, we may not get an opportunity like this again. Don't fight me, darling. I want to make love to you.'

'*No*, Roger!' She moved her head from side to side to evade his searching mouth. 'No, I won't let you.'

His mouth claimed hers with a savagery he had never used before, forcing her lips apart to deepen the kiss. His legs across her knees pinioned her to the bed and her protests went unheard by him, his hands running freely over her body.

'I love you, Alexandra,' he groaned raggedly, his face buried in her hair.

'I'm sure she's glad to hear it,' said a chillingly angry voice. 'But if you don't take your hands off her immediately I may be forced to ram those words down your throat.'

Roger was off the bed in two seconds flat, glaring with resentful anger at Dominic Tempest. 'You have a way of turning up when you're not wanted,' he said nastily, his face flushed.

Dominic looked at him scornfully. 'By the look of it I turned up at exactly the right time. Gail's condition isn't a good excuse for using this house for your assignations.' He looked at Alexandra as she sat pale-faced on the bed. 'I told you about that earlier. I thought you'd taken notice of what I said.'

'I—I did.' Roger's unusual behaviour and the humiliation of being found in such a compromising situation by Dominic Tempest had made her feel ill. 'I did,' she repeated in anguish, unable to look at either of them.

'It damn well looks like it,' Dominic rasped. 'Go on, Alexandra, get back to the house. I'll talk to you later. And I'll thank you for your key to this house.' He held out his hand.

She stood up, reaching with shaking fingers into her denims pocket. 'I—It isn't what you think, Dominic. This has never happened before,' she added pleadingly.

He took the key from her hand. 'I don't suppose it has, not in this house anyway. Gail and Trevor would hardly go out and leave you to it. Now go on home, I want to have a word with your boy-friend.'

Roger put a hand on her arm as she walked past him, her head downbent. 'Alexandra, I——'

She flinched away from him. 'Leave me alone!' She glared at him, huge tears like lakes in her blue eyes. 'Just don't touch me!'

'Alexandra, I didn't mean——'

'I know exactly what you meant to do,' she cried. 'And you won't get a second chance. Goodbye!'

CHAPTER THREE

ALEXANDRA never knew how she managed to drive the car back to the Tempest house, her feelings a mixture of pain and humiliation. Once back in her room she gave in to the threatening tears.

How could Roger, how could he! Oh, he had tried all the usual moves when they had first started going out together, but once she had shown her dislike of a more intimate relationship between them he had treated her with the greatest love and respect.

But this evening he had lost control of his feelings like never before, and she felt sure that if Dominic Tempest hadn't turned up as he had Roger would not have taken no for an answer.

Not that she would have given in to Roger willingly, but already he had been proving the stronger before Dominic had interrupted them. He had never acted like that before, and it had frightened her. She didn't know how she was going to face him again.

She hurriedly wiped the tears away from her cheeks as someone knocked on the door. 'Come in,' she said huskily.

Dominic entered the room. 'Are you all right?' he asked softly.

Perhaps if he hadn't been so gentle with her she would have been all right, but the sympathetic look in his eyes was her undoing. 'Oh, Dominic,' she cried, 'I feel—I feel so degraded!'

He sat down beside her, pulling her into his arms to cradle her head on his shoulder. 'Hey, come on. What's happened to the little firebrand I'm used to?'

Alexandra gulped down the tears. 'She seems to have disappeared.'

'For the moment,' he teased.

She shook in his arms. 'It was all so horrible! If you hadn't come along he would—he would have——'

'He just got carried away with the moment, Alex,' he said gently. 'I spoke to him after you left, I drove him home, actually. He couldn't help himself—you have to expect that when you put temptation in his way.'

'But I—I didn't,' she denied indignantly. 'At least, not intentionally.'

Dominic chuckled. 'I've got news for you. You don't need to do it intentionally.'

She pushed away from him, a new panic entering her eyes. 'Please, I——'

'Calm down, Alexandra,' he ordered sternly. 'I'm the last person you should fear those sort of attentions from. We can't stand each other, remember?'

She gave a shaky smile. 'I'm sorry, my nerves are all shot to pieces. I just didn't expect that sort of behaviour from Roger. I thought he loved me.'

Dominic stood up. 'You really are an innocent, Alex. It's because he believes himself to be in love with you that things got out of hand. At his age you don't have a lot of control, when you get old and ancient like me it takes a little more than a beautiful face and a youthful body to turn you on. And he's very sorry it happened, he did nothing but apologise all the way back to his home. He's suffering, Alex, if that makes you feel any better.'

'It doesn't.'

'I realise he's frightened you,' Dominic said gravely. 'And I realise that what I witnessed tonight had never happened before. You were really upset about it.'

'It was awful!' She couldn't meet his eyes.

'Oh, surely not awful, Alex? After all, if the two of you were married, as you'd wanted to be, you would be on a much more intimate footing.'

'Yes, I know, but it—it wouldn't be the same!'

'Of course it would,' he contradicted. 'Exactly the same. Do you love Roger?'

'You know I do,' she said resentfully.

'And you've never been tempted to go to bed with him?'

She blushed scarlet. 'Never.'

'Then you don't love him,' he stated calmly, reaching for the doorhandle.

'How can you say that?' She stood up. 'How can you possibly know how I feel about him? You couldn't tell that on such short acquaintance.'

Dominic opened the door. 'I wouldn't even need to see him to tell you how you feel about him, the fact that you don't want to sleep with him is enough.'

'I didn't say——'

'You said you've never been tempted to, which amounts to the same thing. It's almost time for dinner, I'll see you later.' He stopped his exit, reaching in his trousers pocket. 'You might as well have your key to the house—after what you've just told me I don't think I have any reason to suspect you of meeting Young there.'

'You——' she began.

'I'll see you at dinner, Alex.'

'I don't think I want any.'

Dominic shrugged. 'Please yourself.'

Her breakfast was doubly welcome the next morning after she had stubbornly refused to go down for dinner the evening before. But at least Dominic wasn't there to witness the enormous meal she ate—that would have been too humiliating.

Gail already looked rested when she visited her that afternoon, a healthy blush to her cheeks. Alexandra put the flowers she had bought her sister on the locker beside the bed, and bent to kiss her cheek. 'You look wonderful.'

Gail blushed. 'Possibly because Trevor has just left.'

Alexandra laughed. 'I see. Say no more. Well, I want you to know that everything is all right back at the house. I went over there yesterday.'

Gail sighed her relief. 'I suddenly thought of the mess I'd left everything in just as I was falling asleep last night. Of course when I told Trevor he said not to worry about it. Typical male! He doesn't seem to realise that you can't just suddenly up and leave a house.'

'Well, now you don't have to worry about it, it's all been taken care of.'

'How are you settling down, living with Dominic?' Gail looked at her interestedly.

Alexandra flushed with feeling. 'Don't put it like that, Gail,' she said abruptly. 'I'm only a guest in his house, a guest he would rather not see too much of.'

'That wasn't what he said this morning.'

'This morning?' she looked sharply at her sister. 'He's already been to see you?'

'Mm, he came in about eleven. He brought the roses. Didn't he tell you he'd been here?'

Alexandra avoided her eyes. 'I—I haven't seen him today.'

Gail raised her eyebrows. 'You didn't have lunch together?'

'Nor breakfast either. Dominic's very busy,' she added hastily 'He has his work to do. He has to go up to London Wednesday and Thursday.'

'Oh yes. He stays overnight, doesn't he?'

So he could be with his mistress for the night! 'Yes. They're lovely flowers that he brought you.' Alexandra changed the subject.

'They come from the garden at his house. It's a lovely house, isn't it?'

'Very nice. I could quite get used to being waited on,' she teased.

'Don't get too used to it,' Gail laughed. 'There'll be plenty to do once I get home with the baby. I wish it could be soon,' she added wistfully. 'I'm getting a little tired of being this size.'

'That's why you're in here, so that you can rest.'

'Mm, but the baby isn't resting, he's more active than ever.'

'You're sure it's a he, then?' Alexandra teased.

Her sister laughed. 'It had better be, or Trevor and Dominic will never forgive me! They both want it to be a boy.'

'Surely it has nothing to do with Dominic,' Alexandra said sharply.

'He will be its uncle,' Gail pointed out gently.

Alexandra gave a harsh laugh. 'Well, I'll be its aunty, but I haven't put in a claim for a girl.'

'Would you like it to be a girl?'

'I don't mind what it is.'

'Neither do I. And Dominic will love the baby no matter what it is, we all will. We're just fed up waiting.'

A nurse put her head round the side of the door. 'Time for your nap, Mrs Tempest,' she said with a smile.

'Can't my sister stay a little while longer?' Gail asked pleadingly.

'I'm afraid not. You've had far too many visitors today already, and I'm sure Dr Tempest will be in again later.' The nurse disappeared again.

Alexandra stood up. 'The nurse is right, Gail—you must rest.'

'I'm not an invalid, and I feel such a fraud taking up this bed.'

'You'll do as you're told,' her husband told her sternly as he came into the room. 'Hello, love,' he greeted Alexandra. 'How's my big brother treating you?'

'Oh, fine,' she answered shortly. 'How are your bachelor quarters?'

He grimaced. 'Don't ask me!'

Gail giggled. 'His feet were cold all night.'

Alexandra laughed, and kissed her sister goodbye. 'I'll be in to see you tomorrow. Is there anything you want me to bring in?'

'I've made a list out somewhere,' she looked about on the locker. 'Ah, here it is,' she checked down the list. 'There's quite a lot there, but as I'm going to be stuck in here for weeks I might as well have my knitting and sewing, otherwise Junior won't have any clothes to wear when he arrives.'

'Oh, I'm sure we could manage to find him a few things,' Alexandra teased.

'I'll have those things anyway, it will give me something to do.'

'I nearly forgot,' Alexandra looked through her handbag. 'I picked up some books for you this morning.'

'Oh lovely,' Gail smiled her thanks.

'Right, well, I'll be on my way.'

'Can you tell Dominic I'll call him tonight?' Trevor requested of her. 'I'm not sure what time.'

'I'll tell him.' If she saw him! So far today she hadn't set eyes on him. 'See you both tomorrow.'

She went straight into the lounge when she reached the house, coming to an abrupt halt as she found her host sitting in there reading the newspaper. 'Hello,' she said curtly.

'Hi.' He didn't put down the newspaper.

'I understand you went to see Gail this morning.'

He nodded absently. 'That's right.'

'I thought you were taking me with you when you went.'

Dominic slowly lowered the newspaper, his eyes sliding insolently over her as she stood a few feet away from him.

Alexandra shifted uncomfortably as his gaze rested on her slender hips in the skin-tight denims before slowly travelling up to her breasts clearly visible in the thin woollen sun-top she wore. His look was blatantly sexual and her cheeks coloured hotly at the question in his eyes.

'I didn't think you wanted to go anywhere with me,' he said finally.

Alexandra dragged her eyes away from the sensuality of his mobile mouth. 'I don't, at least, not particularly. But I'm sure Gail thought it odd.'

He frowned. 'You haven't been worrying her again?' The intimacy of his mood was dispelled as impatience took over.

'No, I haven't,' she answered with her old fight. 'But I didn't tell her what a charming host you're being either.'

'Can I help it if I can't get used to the idea of having an adolescent in my house twenty-four hours a day?' he mocked. 'I'm not used to having females around me day and night, this is basically a male household.'

'I'm so sorry,' she said sarcastically, dropping into an armchair. 'I was under the impression that women were a primary factor in your life.'

'When you're a woman I'll tell you about it,' he told her dryly. 'If you can be shocked by that tame scene I interrupted last night you'd be a hospital case if I went into all the details of just how important women are to me. But I want a woman about only when I want—well, use your imagination a little. Having a female in my home just to look at is a new experience.'

Remembering the way he had looked at her just now she hoped he wouldn't look at her too often. Her legs had felt weak, every nerve in her body aware of him, and for a few brief minutes she had thought of him only as a vitally attractive man and not as her tormenter. But she mustn't ever forget the way he used women or the parting she had witnessed between him and Sabrina Gilbert the morning before.

'I already know the way you use women,' she said tartly.

'Sabrina,' he smiled to himself.

'Exactly!'

'But Sabrina uses me too. She was married, you know, her divorce went through about four months ago. And when you've been married you get used to a certain—relationship.'

Colour flamed anew in Alexandra's cheeks. 'Are you telling me that she—you——'

'We have a mutual sexual need that we satisfy with each other,' he finished for her, his amusement at her horror evident.

'That's disgusting!'

'I suppose to you it must seem that way. But at least this way there's no jealousy or possessiveness.'

'No love either.'

Dominic gave a derisive smile. 'What's love? And don't try to explain it to me, you don't have the faintest idea what you're talking about.'

She gasped indignantly. 'I have a better idea of it than you do!'

'An idea is right. You've been in love with love the last few months, it's a phase all young single girls go through. Marianne was the same, the only trouble being that I believed it to be the real thing. Roger Young is in the same predicament I found myself in fourteen years ago.'

Her mouth tightened. 'I don't want to talk about Roger.'

'Because he dared to show a little passion?' He shook his head. 'That was nothing.'

'Nothing? He—well, he touched me, and—and——'

'It was nothing,' he repeated infuriatingly. 'When you meet a real man you'll know the difference.'

'A real man!' she scorned. 'I suppose you think yourself one.'

'I don't need to, I leave that to other people.'

'I don't think that about you, I just think you're arrogant and boastful.'

His narrowed grey eyes levelled on her critically. 'I think you're being antagonising,' he said thoughtfully. 'Now why could that be?' he mused. 'Could it be that you're curious as to whether or not it would be different with me?'

'No—no, I——' her eyes widened. 'Certainly not!'

He pushed himself to his feet, his muscles rippling beneath the fitted brown shirt he wore, coming to stand in front of her, his eyes challengingly on her bent head. 'I would be more than happy to oblige, Alex,' he said softly.

Alexandra licked her suddenly dry lips, her eyes on a level with the waistband of his trousers. 'Don't be silly! I—I was only——'

'Only trying to force me into this,' he finished. 'I'm perfectly well aware of the look you gave me when you came into the room, and there was nothing innocent about it.'

'The look *I* gave *you*?' Alexandra cut in heatedly, her blue eyes clashing with his cool grey ones. 'It was you— you were mentally undressing me.'

'You're right,' he surprised her by admitting. 'I caught a brief glimpse of your bare midriff when you were with Young and I wanted to know what the rest of you looks like.'

'The same as every other woman!' she snapped in her embarrassment; his admission was the last thing she had been expecting. 'We all have the same anatomy.'

Dominic smiled. 'But some of you have more than others.'

'Are you saying I'm fat?' she asked sharply.

'I didn't mean weight-wise.' His eyes taunted her, the mocking lift to his mouth incensing her even more. He put out a hand and pulled her to her feet, his eyes on her uplifted breasts. 'Certain men prefer certain parts of the female body. Personally, I've always liked these,' his fingertips ran lightly over the tip of her breasts. 'And yours are lovely.'

'Stop it!' Alexandra recoiled away from him. 'How dare you? How dare you talk to me like this, *touch* me like this!'

'I dare because you want me to.'

'I do not!'

'Oh yes, you do, Alex. You're just awakening to the pleasure you can get from your body, and what you shared with Young last night did not give you pleasure. Right now you're wondering if it's the same with every man. I'm offering to prove that it isn't.'

She backed away from him. 'Dominic, don't do this. How can we live together with you acting like this?' she pleaded.

'Quite easily, much easier than we are at the moment.'

'But we—yesterday you said you couldn't stand me.'

'And today I've changed my mind.'

'You can't do that——'

The butler entered the room after a brief knock and Alexandra moved hurriedly to the other side of the room. Dominic had made her aware of him as she had never been aware of any man before, not even Roger. But it was a purely sexual awareness, nothing like her love for Roger.

'Mr Young is on the telephone again for Miss Paige, sir,' Charles informed them.

Roger! Thank heavens, a return to normality after the tenseness of the last few minutes. 'I'll take it in the dining-room, thank you, Charles,' she answered.

Dominic was watching her as the butler left the room.

'Charles informed me earlier that you've been refusing telephone calls from Roger all day. You've suddenly decided to speak to him.'

'Yes. If you'll excuse me.' She made a mad dash for the door.

'You changed your mind because of what happened just now,' he said softly. She wrenched open the door. 'If you must know, yes!'

'Don't think that forgiving your boy-friend will change anything between us,' he warned. 'We're aware of each other now and nothing can change that.'

Standing apart from his disturbing influence some of her fight returned.

'You're just aware of the fact that you have a female living in your house and you think it's too good an opportunity to miss.'

To her chagrin he smiled. 'You can fight me all you want, Alex, but I'll get you in the end, one way or another.'

She looked at him sharply. 'What do you mean, get me?'

Dominic turned away. 'Forget I said it,' he ordered harshly. 'I must be insane. You're half my age, a mere child.'

'Dominic, you——'

'Stay out of my way, Alex!' he snapped. 'Go and talk to your boy-friend and forget this ever happened.'

She leant heavily on the door once she was out of the room. How could she be expected to forget anything that had taken place just now, the things Dominic had said, the way he had touched her? Her body still tingled from that touch and she felt she would never be the same again.

She sounded breathless when she picked up the telephone. 'Roger?' she said tentatively.

'Oh, Alexandra. Thank goodness you're speaking to

me! I've been going frantic today when you wouldn't answer any of my calls.'

Here was a man and a situation she was better able to control. 'You could always have come over, I've been in most of the day.'

'I suggested that earlier when I spoke to Mr Tempest, but he didn't seem to think it a good idea.'

She stiffened. 'You spoke to Dominic?'

'Yes, he said you were at the hospital visiting Gail.'

'But he told you not to come over?' she persisted.

'He said he wasn't sure of your reaction. I'm sorry about last night, I don't know what came over me—well, I do, but I shouldn't——'

All tension left her body. 'Forget it, Roger. I shouldn't have reacted so violently. Dominic coming in like that shook me a little.'

'I felt a little embarrassed myself. I don't think he likes me.'

She gave a shaky laugh. 'He doesn't like me either. He wasn't rude to you, was he?'

'A bit abrupt, but not rude. Will you come over for dinner this evening?' Roger asked hopefully.

'Do your parents know we had an argument?' She couldn't face them if they did, especially if they knew the reason for it—not that it was the sort of thing Roger was likely to tell his parents.

'No, I didn't tell them.'

'In that case, I would love to come over.' Anything to avoid having to sit down to dinner with Dominic Tempest.

'Great. About seven-thirty?'

'Will there be anyone else there?'

'No, just the family.'

'Fine. I'll see you later, then.'

Dominic was just leaving the lounge as Alexandra came out of the dining-room. She coloured immediately, her telephone conversation with Roger not helping to dispel the awareness that had sprung up between herself and Dominic this afternoon.

She knew he was as much aware of it as she was by the wary look in his eyes. They looked at each other across the passageway, neither speaking but the tension between them a tangible thing.

Finally it was Dominic who spoke. 'You made it up with him, then,' he said abruptly.

'Yes. I'm going out to dinner.' She couldn't meet his gaze.

He gave a half smile. 'You didn't need to do that to avoid me. I'll be working through dinner tonight anyway.'

'I didn't do it to avoid you. Why should I?' She looked at him defiantly.

'Why indeed?' he mused.

'Excuse me,' she brushed past him, 'I'm going to my room.'

'You have nothing to fear from me,' he rasped. 'I'll admit to a momentary attraction, but it's passed now. It will never happen again.'

She stopped with her foot on the bottom stair. 'I hope not.'

'Don't hope, Alex, *know*,' he said behind her. 'Perhaps for a moment you reminded me of Marianne, I don't know.'

She spun round to face him, anger in every line of her body. 'Is that supposed to make me feel better, the fact that I was a substitute for your wife?'

'Ex-wife,' he corrected. 'And that wasn't what I meant, all I was trying to explain was that I——'

'Don't bother to finish!' Alexandra snapped. 'You're insulting, do you know that?'

His grey eyes narrowed. 'I wasn't trying to be insulting.'

'You don't need to try!' She ran up the stairs. 'A substitute for your wife!'

'Alex!'

Her blue eyes flashed. 'Don't you "Alex" me! You just carry on your sexual relationship with Sabrina Gilbert and leave me alone. Keep your insults for her—maybe she doesn't mind being used in that way.'

'Alex, will you listen to me!' he commanded angrily.

'No, I won't! And so that the whole house doesn't become aware of just how despicable you are I'll go to my room before I really lose my temper. I'll be glad to get out of this house tonight!' She turned and ran to her room.

She had reminded him of his wife indeed! Had Marianne Tempest looked anything like her?—she didn't remember anyone ever saying she had. She would ask Gail the next time she visited her; she had seen pictures of her. But what an insult!—the attraction Dominic had felt hadn't even been for her.

There was a hammering on her bedroom door. 'Alex? Alex, let me in!' It was Dominic, and he sounded really angry. Thank goodness she had thought to lock the door.

'Why? So that you can imagine I'm your wife again?' She slammed shut her wardrobe door after taking out the gown to wear that evening. 'No, thank you!'

'It wasn't like that,' his voice lowered. 'I was just trying to make you feel better when I said that.'

'Feel better!' she cried. 'To be told I reminded you of another woman was supposed to make me feel better?'

'You're deliberately misunderstanding me,' he said impatiently. 'Open the door,' he rattled the door-handle.

'I'm taking a shower, Dominic.'

A short silence. 'All the more reason to open the door,' he suggested throatily.

'Go to hell!'

She could hear him laughing. 'Okay, Alex, please yourself. Have a nice time this evening.'

'I will!'

She would make sure she did if only to spite him, and she would have done if it wasn't for the fact that as soon as she saw Roger she knew things were over between them. Whatever love she had thought she felt for him no longer existed, only liking and friendship were left.

The knowledge held her tongue-tied all through dinner. She was here under false pretences, the Youngs believing her to be their future daughter-in-law. But she couldn't marry Roger now; she didn't love him.

What would she have done if they had already been married? How disastrous that would have been. And she probably would have been married to him too if it weren't for Dominic's interference; she could have persuaded Gail and Trevor around to her way of thinking if it hadn't been for him, she knew that now.

It was the reason for discovering her infatuation and not love for Roger that worried her the most. Perhaps it was the fact that she could feel drawn to Dominic that had prompted this change of heart, but whatever it was she didn't know what to do about it.

Roger was still in love with her, it had been apparent when he had kissed her on her arrival. She still felt pleasure in his embrace, but it was no longer the same, there had been none of the tingling excitement she usually felt.

They went up to Roger's sitting-room after dinner to play records. 'You're very quiet,' Roger remarked concernedly.

She gave a bright smile. 'Sorry, I didn't mean to be.'

'You're not still mad at me, are you?' He came to sit next to her on the sofa. 'I thought you'd forgiven me.'

'There was nothing to forgive,' she said nervously. 'I was just being silly.'

'Kiss and make up?' he asked persuasively.

She gave a light laugh to cover her aversion to such an act. 'Not just now, Roger. Let's listen to the records.'

'I'd much rather kiss you,' he said sulkily.

'After last night I think we should calm things down a little,' she snapped. 'Just be friends for a while.'

He lifted her chin, searching her face for some sign of teasing. 'You are joking, darling?' he asked uncertainly.

'No,' she pushed back her long hair from her face, 'I'm confused, Roger. I don't know what I want any more.' Except that she no longer wanted to marry him.

He shook his head. 'I don't understand you.'

Alexandra smoothed the frown from his brow. 'I don't understand myself.'

'But we're getting engaged soon, Gail and Trevor agreed that we could when you were seventeen and a half. I thought we could go and look for a ring at the weekend.'

Alexandra stood up. 'No, not this weekend! I—I have too much to think about with Gail in hospital.'

Roger watched her closely. 'That isn't the reason. I have apologised for last night, Alexandra, I can't do any more.'

'I accepted that apology. It's just that last night proved to me that I'm not ready for marriage.' She looked at him pleadingly. 'Surely you've realised that too?'

'I know that last night unnerved you. But that was only because we aren't married yet. Of course you couldn't let me make love to you then, I was being stupid to expect it. But once we're married——'

'No!' she denied sharply. 'I can't marry you. I can't!'

Roger wasn't quick enough to stop her exit and she managed to get almost to the front door of the house before anyone stopped her.

'Are you leaving, my dear?' Mrs Young came out of the lounge.

'Er—Yes. I—I—Mr Tempest doesn't like me to be in late,' Alexandra said hurriedly.

'Quite right of him. It's very thoughtful of you to consider his feelings like this. I'll wish you goodnight, Alexandra.'

'Goodnight, Mrs Young.' She left quickly as she saw Roger starting to descend the stairs.

The light was still on in Dominic's study as she crept into the house and so she made as little noise as possible on her way up the stairs. Nevertheless, she must have made some noise because she heard the study door open and turning she saw Dominic looking up at her.

'You're home early,' he remarked thoughtfully.

'Yes.'

'You didn't enjoy your evening?'

'Yes, yes, I did,' she contradicted. 'I—er—I'm rather tired, that's all,' she lied.

'I see. You forgot to tell me Trevor would be telephoning tonight.'

'I'm sorry,' she said abruptly.

'It didn't matter, I was in all evening anyway.'

She turned to leave. 'Goodnight, Dominic.'

'I'm going to London in the morning,' he said softly behind her.

That stopped her progress and she turned back to face him. 'But it's only Tuesday,' she exclaimed.

'Yes, but I think it best. It will give you a few days to get over the situation I've created here.'

'So you admit there is a situation,' she scoffed.

'It would be useless to deny it. I'm aware of you and you're aware of me, and it's better if we don't see each other for a few days.' He shrugged. 'I'm hoping things will be different when I get back.'

'When you've spent a few days with your mistress,'

she accused fiercely. Dominic sighed. 'Yes.'

'Does she know she's a substitute too?' she sneered. 'Does she know that you're thinking of someone else as you make love to her? I'm sure that even with the casual relationship you say you have with her she wouldn't stand for that.'

His face was thunderous. 'I have never thought of any-one else when I make love to her!' he denied furiously.

'Not even Marianne?' she taunted.

'Especially Marianne!'

Alexandra looked at him suspiciously. 'Why do you say that?'

'Because Marianne means nothing to me, she didn't long before our marriage broke up. She's married to some other poor idiot now and I hope they're happy together.'

'You don't care for her?'

'No,' he said simply.

'But you said—you said——' her voice broke. 'I hate you!'

'I hope you do,' he accepted with a sigh. 'Your hate I can take, it would be your love that would break me.'

'I don't love *you*!'

'Good, let's keep it that way. I'll see you some time Thursday or Friday.' He turned to re-enter his study.

'I hope you never come back!' she shouted at him childishly.

He looked up at her. 'Oh, I'll be back. I may even dance at your wedding when the time comes, but until it does stay out of my way. I've never taken another man's wife and it may be the only thing that will save you.'

'From you?'

He nodded. 'From me. Goodnight, Alex.'

She didn't correct him over the use of her name. 'Goodnight,' she said huskily before running up to her room.

CHAPTER FOUR

SHE called Roger the next morning and apologised for running out on him. They arranged to meet for lunch at a restaurant in town, Alexandra knowing that she had to talk her uncertainty over with Roger. He wasn't going to like it, but it would at least explain her strange moods towards him of late.

'So you don't want to marry me?' He paused in the eating of his meal, the restaurant they had chosen quite busy.

Alexandra looked around her self-consciously, hoping no one else could hear their conversation. 'I'm saying that I'm unsure, and if I'm unsure it's best to wait.'

'Does your living with Dominic Tempest have anything to do with this uncertainty?' he asked crossly.

'I'm not living with him!' she burst out, her face fiery red. 'Why do people keep saying that,' she snapped.

'Who else has said it?' Roger asked suspiciously.

'Just Gail.'

'She probably said it because she's noticed the change in you too.'

'Don't talk rubbish, Roger, I haven't changed.'

He shook his head. 'I'm not the one talking rubbish. Do you imagine yourself in love with Tempest, is that it?'

Alexandra gave up all pretence of eating. 'How can you even suggest such a thing? You know I can't stand the man.'

'I also know that it's since you've been living with him that you've changed towards me. I made a move on Sunday evening that I admit was a little stupid, but once upon a time you would have shrugged off a situation like that. Heavens, it wasn't the first time I've tried to go a bit too far. So why make such a big thing out of it this time?'

She sighed at his lack of understanding. 'I'm trying to explain it to you, Roger, but you just won't listen.'

'I am listening, it just doesn't seem to make sense.'

'It doesn't make sense because you won't let me finish,' she snapped impatiently. 'I'm uncertain about marriage between us *because* I reacted so violently about Sunday night. Don't you see, if I was in love with you I would have wanted you to make love to me, whether we were married or not.'

He put his hand over hers, squeezing gently. 'You wouldn't, Alexandra. You're much too innocent for that.'

She looked at him eagerly. 'Do you really think that's the reason? Really?'

He smiled at her. 'Of course it is—you aren't the type of girl to enter into an affair, and we both know that we can't marry for another six months. What if we should make a slip-up? It would ruin everything.'

Alexandra was scarlet by this time. 'We've never discussed this sort of thing before. I—it——'

'It's embarrassing, I know. But it's something we should have talked about, made our feelings clear on the subject.'

'That's a bit clinical, isn't it?' she asked huskily.

'Maybe, but it would save a lot of trouble in the long run. I love you, Alexandra, and I want to make love to you,' Roger said earnestly. 'But I want you for my wife, and I can wait until then.'

So could she—that was the trouble. There was none of the desperation she would have expected, none of the tense excitement she had felt when Dominic Tempest had only looked at her.

But that could have been due to his age and experience. Dominic was every woman's challenge, the unattainable, and for a while yesterday she had been tempted to accept his challenge. But Dominic wasn't reality, Roger could give her that, and she had nearly given him up!

'Oh, Roger,' she choked, 'I've been so stupid. I don't know what came over me.' Except Dominic Tempest, and he wasn't even worth thinking about. She would simply ignore anything he said to her in future.

'Nerves, darling. It's only natural.'

She laughed. 'We aren't getting married for months yet.'

'So we'll go and look at rings on Saturday?' he persisted.

'Just to look,' she warned. 'I couldn't possibly get engaged while Gail is in hospital. We'll have to have a party, and we can't do that until she gets home.'

He couldn't hide his disappointment. 'But that's weeks away!'

Dear Roger! How could she have possibly have doubted she loved him? 'Never mind, pet, perhaps Gail will have the baby early.'

'I hope so.'

She laughed. 'So does she!'

'My mother and father have—well, they've suggested that they convert the top of the house into a self-contained flat for us.' Roger looked at her hopefully.

Alexandra felt her heart sink. She liked Roger's parents, but she didn't want to live with them. They were inclined to spoil Roger and she didn't think marriage would change their attitude. She felt her uncertainty returning.

'Do you think that's a good idea?' she asked evasively.

'Well, I—— Look, shall we get out of here, go to the park where we can talk more privately?'

'Yes,' she agreed gratefully, 'I think that's a good idea.'

She waited in the reception area while Roger paid their bill and then they walked the short distance to the park. Alexandra smiled at the antics of the young ducks on the pond as they clambered all over their quacking mother.

'Aren't they cute?' she mused.

'Yes.' Roger was preoccupied. 'Let's sit on that bench over there.'

She did as he asked, knowing he was anxious to get back to the question of the converted flat, and she didn't know how she was going to say no without stepping on too many toes.

'You don't like the idea, do you?' he said suddenly.

'Oh, Roger, it isn't that. I just——'

'We all thought it was the ideal solution,' he cut in. 'We obviously can't afford a house of our own.'

'You've already discussed it with your parents?' She couldn't hide her dismay.

'Well, they did suggest it yesterday, but as you know I didn't get a chance to talk to you about it last night. The idea is to convert the very top floor of the house into a flat for us. It will need a lot of work to make it self-contained, that's why they're suggesting it now.'

'But we agreed we were going to rent a flat for a while, until we can afford to buy a house of our own.'

'That could be never,' Roger scorned. 'It will be years until I'll be earning that sort of money.'

'But living with your parents! That's almost as bad as living with Gail and Trevor. We wouldn't have any privacy.' She knew Roger's parents, they might make the flat self-contained but no doubt they would more often than not expect them to dine downstairs with them.

Roger's mouth tightened. 'Of course we would—the flat would be ours. Much better than renting some scruffy dump that will probably be damp, because on the money I get that's about all I could afford.'

Alexandra knew he was talking sense, but she also knew that they weren't his own words, they were obviously the facts his parents had put forward in their argument. She could see the sense of what was being said—but she wouldn't live with her in-laws!

'We have months to think about this, Roger,' she insisted.

'Not really. As I said, the work on the conversion would have to start soon.'

'But not yet,' she said lightly. 'Let me think about it, Roger. It's a serious decision to make.' And one she didn't even want to make.

'Okay.' He seemed satisfied with this. 'Are you visiting Gail this afternoon?'

'Yes, I have to take some things in to her.' She grimaced. 'She wants her knitting.'

'From the house?'

'Mm, she gave me a list of things to take to her.'

'I thought Tempest had taken your key away.'

Alexandra blushed as she remembered the circumstances behind him doing such a thing—and the reason he had given it back to her. 'He changed his mind. After all, it is my home.'

'Would you like me to come to the hospital with you?' asked Roger. 'I'd like to see Gail.'

She laughed. 'I'm sure she would like to see you too, anything for a new face.'

'Charming!' He pulled her to her feet. 'Come on then, let's go.'

They stopped off briefly at the house to pick up the things on Gail's mammoth list.

'We'll probably have a heatwave,' Alexandra joked to Gail, 'with all these cardigans you keep knitting the baby.'

'I hope not,' Gail grimaced. 'It's already hot in here, I don't think I could stand a heatwave as well. I'm sure they've got the heating on, and it's the middle of summer!'

'It's for the babies, not for you.'

'Well, I'm baking.' She sprayed some perfume on herself. 'They say I'm here to rest and yet they wake me up at six o'clock with a cup of tea, the morning routine and doctors' round stop you sleeping in the morning, and then they keep feeding you and giving you cups of tea and throwing vitamins down you at odd hours of the day.'

'And in the afternoon you get people visiting you and keeping you awake,' Alexandra finished with a laugh. 'I think we should go, Roger.'

'Don't you dare,' Gail threatened. 'You're the only thing that's keeping me sane. I'd much rather be at home.'

'We would rather have you there too,' Alexandra said gently. 'I'm at home all the time now, couldn't they let me take care of you?'

'Trevor's going to talk to Dr Jenner about it, but I hope I can, and soon.'

'I'm perfectly capable of looking after you, and I don't like having to stay at Dominic's.' Even more so after yesterday.

'Trevor says he's gone to London.'

'Has he?' Roger looked surprised. 'You didn't tell me that, darling.'

Alexandra shrugged. 'I didn't think it was important.'

'But you're all alone there now.'

'Hardly alone—Dominic has lots of servants. Besides, he said he'd be back before the end of the week. I'll hardly know he's gone. Maybe we'll have Gail out of here by then and I can move back to care for her.'

'But Dominic doesn't usually leave until Wednesday,'

Gail said thoughtfully.

Alexandra grinned. 'Maybe I drove him away,' she teased, hoping they wouldn't guess that was what had actually happened.

'I doubt it,' Gail laughed. 'He's probably had an urgent call from the studio.'

Alexandra looked sharply at her sister. 'You mean he may have gone away on one of his wild assignments?' She couldn't keep the fear out of her voice.

'No, I don't think so. He would have said so. No, it was probably just something to do with the programme.'

It had nothing to do with the programme and everything to do with her. All the more reason for her to get back to the sanity of living with Gail and Trevor. She certainly didn't want any more scenes with Dominic like yesterday, it unsettled her too much.

'That's probably it,' she agreed. 'It seems to keep him pretty busy.'

Roger looked at his watch. 'I have to leave now, but I'm glad to see you're feeling better,' he said to Gail. 'See you tonight, darling?'

'I'll come with you now, before I get thrown out.' Alexandra stood up too. 'You get some sleep now, Gail, and I'll be in again tomorrow.'

'These damned doctors and their rest,' Gail mumbled.

Alexandra laughed. 'Get on with your knitting. The baby should have about fifteen matinee jackets by the time you're finished.'

'Stop teasing me. I have to do something to pass the time.'

'Well, you will have these babies.'

'Baby! It's going to be the singular—I hope.'

'Knowing your luck ...' Alexandra teased again.

Gail pulled a face. 'That's all I need.'

Alexandra bent to kiss her sister. 'See you tomorrow, love. And give my love to Trevor.'

'They appear to be looking after her,' said Roger once they were outside.

'Oh, they are, but it's an awful long time to just sit there waiting.'

'Mr Tempest left rather suddenly, didn't he?' Roger remarked casually.

Alexandra looked away. 'Urgent business.'

'It must have been, he didn't say anything about it on Sunday. He leads a really strange life, doesn't he, never knowing from one day to the next whether he's going to be sent to the far ends of the earth.'

'Not this time,' she denied quickly.

'No, but he does go away a lot.'

'You sound envious,' she said, watching him closely.

He looked really boyish at that moment. 'Well ... He does lead a pretty exciting life. Any man would envy him.'

'I'm sure your father wouldn't be pleased to hear that, it isn't the way he would expect a budding lawyer to talk. You're supposed to be very staid and respectable, not longing to rush off to troubled places. Besides, it isn't the sort of job a man with views to marriage should be thinking of. It's only because Dominic is totally selfish that he's managed to make a success of it for so long. If he ever loved anyone but himself he wouldn't be able to do it.'

'You've just managed to convince me that you still hate him,' Roger grinned.

'Did you ever doubt it?' She hoped he hadn't, but she certainly had, she still did! He might be miles away, but she could still feel the way he had looked at her, the way she had reacted to him, and still be disturbed by the fact.

Roger hugged her to him. 'Only for a while. You have to admit he's a handsome devil.'

'Yes,' she agreed abruptly. 'But I'm sure that too many women have thought that in the past for him to be interested in someone as naïve as me.'

'I should hope so,' he said indignantly. 'You're my girl. Shall we go out tonight or would you like to come over to my house?'

Remembering the threat of the converted flat Alexandra thought it better if she didn't see Roger's parents for a while; she knew how Mrs Young manoeuvred people without them even being aware of it. Perhaps if she didn't see them for a while they might forget about it.

'Why don't you come over to Dominic's?' she suggested. 'We could have more privacy there now he's away.'

He had a wicked look in his eyes. 'Is that a good idea?'

'Roger!' she gave him a reproachful look.

'Will he mind us being there?'

'He won't know. And he did say that as long as he doesn't keep tripping over my friends I can have over who I want.'

'Hey, that's great, we can have a party.'

She frowned. 'I don't think we should do that, it wouldn't be nice in his absence.'

Roger grasped her forearms. 'But that's the ideal time. It doesn't have to be a real party, just invite a few of the gang over.'

'Let me think about it, maybe tomorrow night.'

He kissed her briefly on the mouth. 'You've got a lot to think about.'

More than even he knew! 'I'll see you later. Come over about eight-thirty.'

Charles provided her with tea when she returned to the house. This brief period of time gave her chance to try and sort herself out. She had allowed Roger to talk her out of cancelling all thoughts of marriage, but what would happen when Dominic returned and his magnetism began to work on her again?

She really shouldn't allow him to get to her like this, it would all be a game to him. But he had taken it seriously enough to have to leave for London a day early! It gave her a strange thrill to be able to unnerve him like that, quite flattering really.

But it shouldn't be! Why should she be flattered because a selfish devil like Dominic Tempest had momentarily found her attractive? She could answer her own question. He was a well-known television personality, worldly and experienced, and he breathed excitement.

That was what had temporarily blinded her to the stupidity of such an attraction, had made her forget her dislike of him, the dislike and anger she had felt towards him most of her life. But she didn't dislike him any more, and that was something she didn't want to probe too deeply.

Charles showed Roger into the lounge that evening with all the stiff politeness he could muster. He apparently didn't approve of his master's young guest entertaining a man here. Alexandra was surprised at his attitude, considering Dominic's morals. But perhaps it was one rule for Dominic and another for her. Well, Charles needn't have worried in that direction; Roger was only here for a drink and a chat, quite innocent compared with Dominic's behaviour.

'He's a real little watchdog, isn't he?' Roger grimaced at Charles' retreating back. 'He more or less gave me the third degree on the doorstep!'

Alexandra laughed, standing up to pour Roger a drink. 'He's just being protective.'

'If it wasn't for the fact that he was so polite about his questioning I could have got quite insulted.'

She sat next to him on the sofa, curling her feet up underneath her. 'Just forget him,' she snuggled against him. 'You're here to be with me.'

'Mm,' he bent to kiss her.

The door opened without warning. 'Excuse me,' Charles interrupted them. 'There is a telephone call for you, Miss Paige.'

Alexandra scrambled to her feet, her face scarlet. She really didn't like the way the telephone calls went through to the servants' quarters to be put through to the main part of the house if necessary. Only having lived in a small household she found this a strange practice, although Dominic probably received telephone calls from numerous fans, and he couldn't talk to them all. There could be no doubt in her mind that Charles would know how to deal with any unwanted callers.

She pushed her dark hair back behind her ears. 'Could you put it through in here, please, Charles.'

'Certainly.'

'Er—Charles,' she halted him. 'Who is it?' she asked belatedly.

'It's Mr Tempest, Miss Paige.'

'Oh, fine,' she smiled. She turned to Roger once the butler had left. 'Perhaps he's found out if he can get Gail discharged.'

'I'm liking the idea more every minute,' said Roger. 'I don't feel comfortable visiting you here.'

Alexandra picked the telephone up as it rang. 'It's lovely to hear from you, Trevor.'

'Perhaps it would be, if it were Trevor,' drawled Dominic.

Her heart leapt. 'Oh.' She hadn't thought of the other 'Mr Tempest', fool that she was.

'Surprised to hear from me?' he continued in that deep sexy voice.

She looked over at Roger, smiling at him reassuringly. 'Yes.'

'Are you pleased I've called?' he asked softly.

'Yes—No! I don't know,' she finished weakly, all too much aware of Roger being in the same room, and the fact that for all her straight thinking earlier just the sound of Dominic's voice over the telephone was enough to put her into a panic.

'Make up your mind, Alex,' he taunted. 'I know I'm pleased to hear your voice. I'm missing you,' he added seductively soft.

'You are?' she squeaked. 'I mean, are you?'

'Mm, strange, isn't it,' he mused. 'For years you've been Trevor's troublesome sister-in-law and in two days that's all changed. I wish now that I hadn't left.'

'But you said—you said——' she looked nervously at Roger as he browsed through some records. 'You know what you said.'

'I said that if I didn't leave things might get a little out of control between us.'

'Yes,' she said breathlessly.

'Since being here I've been wondering if that would be such a bad thing. Alex. I——'

'Is there anything wrong, Alexandra?' Roger came to stand beside her. 'There's nothing wrong with Gail, is there?'

Her eyes flew to his face in a panic. He still believed this call to be from Trevor! 'No, nothing is wrong. Help yourself to another drink, I won't be a moment.'

'Is Young there with you?' Dominic rasped down the telephone. 'Alex, do you have Young there?'

She trembled at the anger in his voice. 'Yes.'

'So you're taking advantage of my absence to go to bed with him,' he accused.

The telephone shook in her hand. 'No, I——'

'Forget it, Alex. Forget I rang.' The line went dead as he slammed down the telephone.

It took her several seconds to gather her thoughts together. She put the receiver slowly back on its cradle.

What did it all mean? Why had Dominic really telephoned her? She would probably never know now.

'Are you sure everything is all right?' Roger probed beside her. 'You look a bit upset.'

She wasn't surprised—she was upset, and utterly confused. Dominic had been about to say something important and Roger had stopped him by interrupting. 'Everything is fine,' she told him vaguely.

'What did Trevor have to say?'

'Trevor?' she asked sharply. 'Oh, he—he just wanted to make sure I was all right.' Now why had she lied? She should have told him it was Dominic. But could she really have told him anything about the conversation? Hardly! But she didn't like deceiving him like this, and she resented Dominic for forcing her to do so.

Roger nodded understandingly. 'Because his brother is away, I suppose.'

If they only knew, they had more to fear for her safety when Dominic *was* here. He was a threat to everything she held dear. She had been managing to maintain some degree of normality before his telephone call and now she was confused again, unsure of herself as only he could make her.

'Probably,' she agreed abruptly. 'About that party, Roger,' she changed the subject, 'I suppose we could invite about a dozen or so people over tomorrow, if you still want to.'

He grinned. 'Oh, I want to. I can hardly wait to see Charles' face when he had to show your guests in. You have to invite Solly. If he doesn't make the snooty butler lose his cool then nothing will.'

Solly was a friend of theirs who always dressed in 'teddy-boy' gear, from his thick crepe-soled shoes to his shoelace tie, and Alexandra thought it would be funny to see Charles' reaction to him too.

For the next hour they telephoned round to their

friends, although she had no intention of letting to-morrow night's gathering turn into one of the rowdy parties they usually went to. This wasn't her home and she probably wouldn't even have thought about inviting these people here if Dominic hadn't upset her again.

It was after ten o'clock when Trevor arrived, and Alexandra felt her heart sink at the sight of him. She just hoped he wouldn't say anything to give away the fact that he hadn't called her earlier. She should have realised that the way her luck was running lately that would be an impossibility.

'Hi,' he kissed her cheek. 'Sorry it's so late, but I was working.'

'That's all right. Sit down. Would you like something to eat or drink?' she asked brightly, a little tenseness about her.

'No, thanks, I've already eaten. Gail seemed concerned about you, so I promised her I would come over and see how you are.' He sat down.

Alexandra shook her head. 'She never stops fretting, does she?'

'She never will, not until you're married, and maybe not even then. How are you, Roger?' he smiled at the younger man.

'I'm fine.' Roger looked puzzled. 'Didn't you telephone earlier?'

'Me? No.' Now it was Trevor's turn to look puzzled. 'I would have done, but we had an emergency in. Anyway, Gail wanted me to actually come here. She thought Alexandra might be lonely,' he added teasingly.

'So you didn't telephone earlier?' Roger repeated, looking accusingly at Alexandra.

'No.'

'I see.' Roger bit his bottom lip. 'Alexandra?' he queried sharply.

She had been holding her breath all this time and now

it was released with a hiss. 'Yes?' she delayed.

'Was the telephone call from Trevor's brother?'

She sighed. 'It—well, it——'

'Was it?' he demanded tightly.

She chewed on her bottom lip. 'Yes.'

He sprang out of the chair, anger in every line of his body. 'You lied to me! You do have something going with him, that's why you answered in monosyllables.'

'What are you talking about?' Trevor frowned at the two of them.

'What am *I* talking about?' Roger gave a sharp laugh. 'I'm talking about your brother and Alexandra. I'm talking about the affair the two of them are having!'

Trevor looked at Alexandra as she gasped, slowly turning back to face Roger. 'Have you been drinking?'

'I wish to God I had,' Roger said bitterly. 'You've really taken me for a fool, Alexandra. I bet the only reason you called me to apologise this morning was because you had to allay suspicions about the two of you. After all, it is rather disgusting, isn't it, a man of thirty-four and a young girl of seventeen. So disgusting that even he's ashamed of it!'

'You're wrong, Roger. Dominic isn't——'

He nodded. 'Oh yes, he is. It all adds up now—your aversion to me on Sunday, the way you're suddenly un-sure about the wedding, the way you lied just now about his telephone call. You've been playing me along, pre-tending all this time that you hated the man when you were really carrying on with him behind my back!'

'Roger, please don't continue this,' she pleaded. 'You're wrong, so wrong.'

'I'm through being your shield in all this. I don't ever want to see you again.'

'After the way you've just spoken to her you won't be allowed to,' Trevor cut in harshly. 'Just stay away from her.'

'I intend to,' Roger sneered, slamming out of the room.

'Sit down, Alexandra,' Trevor said gently. 'I want to talk to you.'

She did as he asked, wringing her hands together. 'It wasn't like he said, Trevor,' she said almost pleadingly.

'Tell me what it is like. He seemed pretty sure about you and Dominic.'

'You don't believe him!'

He shrugged. 'Should I?'

'No! He's acting ridiculously. You know how I've always felt towards Dominic.'

'*Did* Dom telephone you earlier?' he queried softly.

She paled. 'Yes.'

'And why didn't you tell Roger it was him?'

'Because he assumed it was you. And because— because——'

'And because it wasn't the sort of conversation you could tell him about,' Trevor finished for her. 'Has Dom been making passes at you?'

'Hardly!'

'Don't pretend with me, Alexandra, I've known you since you wore braces on your teeth. You're a bundle of nerves the last few days—and now I know the reason why. My own brother!' he swore angrily. 'I thought even he had some decency left in him. Well, that settles it—you're moving back home, gossip or no gossip. I would rather have people talking about the two of us than you having to fight off my brother day and night.'

'It isn't like that.'

'Not at the moment, maybe, but when he gets back he'll set out to win you and then he'll tire of you like he does all the rest. I won't let him use you in that way,' he vowed angrily. 'You can move out of here tomorrow.' He shook his head. 'I wouldn't have believed he could stoop so low.'

'He hasn't, Trevor. Roger was imagining things.'

'Maybe he was and maybe he wasn't, but I'm aware of the danger now and I'm going to stop things before they go any further.'

'They haven't *gone* anywhere,' she said impatiently. 'Dominic isn't interested in me. Oh, he may have flirted with me a little, but that's all.'

'It's enough,' Trevor looked grim. 'You move back to the house tomorrow.'

'Oh, Trevor!' she pouted.

'I mean it.'

'But Dominic isn't even here at the moment. And I have some people coming over tomorrow. Can't I come back on Thursday instead?'

'All right,' he gave in grudgingly. 'Maybe by that time I'll have been able to do something about getting Gail home. At the moment my only leverage is that they need the bed. Okay, you have until Thursday, but no longer.'

She thought about cancelling her get-together all the next day, knowing that everyone would wonder at Roger's absence. But it had to be faced some time, better to get it over with now.

Many more people turned up than had been invited, everyone seeming to invite someone else, until the room was overflowing with people. She had had a feeling it would turn out like this somehow, but she didn't really mind. One girl was conspicuous by her absence, the flirtatious Janey.

'Where's Janey tonight?' Alexandra asked one of the boys, all of them drinking the beer or wine they had brought with them.

John looked uncomfortable. 'I—er—I think she had a previous date.'

'But last night she—— Oh!' she blushed. 'Oh, I see.' Roger hadn't wasted much time in finding someone new.

She couldn't blame him, she would have done the same thing herself if the positions had been reversed.

John put an arm about her shoulders. 'Don't worry about Roger, you still have me.'

She pushed him away laughingly. 'That's what I'm afraid of! I'll go and put some music on.'

'Oh, great! If we move the furniture back we can all dance.'

Alexandra frowned. 'Oh, I don't think so, John. This is Dominic Tempest's house, not mine.'

'Don't be such a spoilsport! Put the records on, we'll behave ourselves.'

Dominic's record collection was quite varied in taste and she found some really recent L.P.s amongst them. Everyone did as they promised, no one drank too much and no one behaved outrageously, and she thought the evening was turning out to be quite a success until she turned to see Dominic standing in the doorway, his face grim as he scrutinised the people in the room.

Alexandra moved hurriedly across the room as Dominic turned on his heel and walked away. She caught up with him just as he reached the top of the stairs. 'Dominic? Dominic, speak to me! It was only a little party, everyone was behaving perfectly,' she added pleadingly.

He shook off her hand, not slackening his pace one little bit as he hurried to his bedroom. 'I couldn't give a damn whether they were or they weren't.' He pulled a case out of his wardrobe, opening the lid to check its contents before snapping it shut again. 'Get out of my way, Alex. I'm in a hurry.'

'Where are you going?' Her mouth felt dry and she licked her lips nervously.

'I can't tell you that,' he snapped.

'You're going on one of your assignments?' She felt

her heart quicken as she waited for his answer.

'Yes.'

'Oh God, Dominic!' She fell into his arms. 'Oh, Dominic, *no!*'

CHAPTER FIVE

HE pushed her roughly away from him. 'What do you mean, no?' He unlocked a drawer at his bedside, pulling out a folder. 'I have a job to do.'

Alexandra shook her head, tears brimming up into her eyes. 'I don't want you to go, Dominic. You could get hurt.'

'I could get hurt crossing the road,' he taunted. 'Go back down to your guests, Alex. I'm sure they're wondering where you are, especially the faithful Roger.'

'He isn't faithful any more.'

His grey eyes narrowed. 'What do you mean?'

'He finished with me last night,' she told him. 'He said he wouldn't be a party to shielding my affair with you any longer.'

'Young fool,' Dominic muttered. 'Doesn't he know an innocent when he sees one?'

'There's something else I think you should know.' Alexandra took a deep breath. 'He said it to Trevor.'

That stopped his movements. 'What the hell did he do that for?' he growled.

'To get back at me, I suppose,' she said impatiently. 'Please, Dominic, tell me where you're going. Is it dangerous?' she added tremulously.

He shrugged. 'I don't know that yet. All I know is that I have a car waiting for me outside and a plane waiting at a local airport to fly me out of the country.'

Her eyes widened. 'Out of the country? But—but where?'

'I already told you that isn't for public knowledge—and that includes you. Watch the programme tomorrow,' he advised. 'Then you'll know all about it.'

'But, Dominic,' she pleaded, 'you can't just leave like this. I won't let you!'

'And how do you propose to stop me?' he asked tauntingly.

'Any way I can,' she told him fiercely.

Dominic stood back challengingly. 'You can try,' he invited softly. 'Well?' he mocked as she hesitated. 'I'm waiting.'

Alexandra hesitated only a moment longer before moving forward to press herself against him, her hands moving up over his chest to pull his head down to her, her lips pressed against his unresponsive ones.

She moved her mouth against his, willing him to show in some way that he wasn't immune to her, that the attraction he hadn't hidden from her before he left for London was still as strong as ever. As hers was!

But he didn't move; his body remained taut and un-yielding, his arms hung limp as his sides. Her hands were threaded through the thickness of his blond hair as she tried even more desperately to evoke a response in him.

Finally she looked up at him. 'Dominic,' she choked, her eyes deeply blue. 'Dominic, please. *Please!*'

'Please, what?' he asked tightly. 'Be very sure before you answer that. I'm not Roger Young.'

'I don't want you to be,' she denied quickly. 'Don't leave me, Dominic,' she begged brokenly. 'Please, I just want you to stay with me. I don't want you to be in danger. Oh, Dominic, please!'

'Dear God!' he groaned, his arms passing about her slim waist to gather her to him, his face buried in the dark thickness of her hair. 'I've thought of nothing but holding you like this since Sunday afternoon when I found you in Young's arms by that tennis court!' He placed fevered kisses on her throat. 'I could have rammed his teeth down his throat for touching you like that. So I was cruel to you instead. You were no more responsible for Gail's collapse than I was, but I wanted to hit out at someone,' he growled. 'You were the obvious choice.'

'Kiss me, Dominic. You've never kissed me.'

He gave a short laugh. 'I've never wanted to until the last few days.'

'And you do now?' Oh God, she hoped so. She had never wanted anything this badly. She had known as soon as he said he was going away, possibly into danger, that her feelings for him had changed drastically in the last few days, that she couldn't let him go away without showing him in some way the extent of this change of feelings.

She loved him, loved him as he had once said she would when she genuinely fell in love. What she had felt for Roger was only a pale shadow of the turmoil she felt in Dominic's arms.

His grey eyes held her mesmerised. 'Oh yes, I want to. But I don't think I should.'

'Not even if I want you to?'

'Especially if you want me to.' He smoothed back her hair from her face, cradling each side of her face. 'You have the most beautiful, tempting blue eyes I've ever seen,' he said huskily. 'I wonder why I've never noticed that before.'

'Possibly because they were usually spitting dislike at you,' she suggested shyly.

'You're probably right,' he agreed. 'But they aren't spitting dislike now, are they?'

'No,' she admitted softly.

Dominic moved away from her, a grim look on his face. 'I can't kiss you, don't you understand. If I do that I shall know, and I—don't want to know.'

Alexandra frowned. 'Don't want to know what?'

'I don't like emotional entanglements,' he said sharply,

determinedly not looking at her. 'I've explained my relationship with Sabrina to you, it means nothing to either of us. And that's the way I like things.'

'Are you saying——' she swallowed hard. 'Are you saying I don't mean anything to you either?'

'No!' he turned on her fiercely. 'No, I'm not saying that at all. God, Alex, I came back here tonight because I—— Oh, hell, forget it!'

'Why did you come back, Dominic?' she asked.

'Because I wanted to see you before I left. I wanted to—to say goodbye to you. And that's quite something, considering I don't like goodbyes. I learnt early on that it's better to just go.'

'From Marianne?' she prompted gently.

'Yes. I shouldn't have come here tonight, you would have learnt soon enough that I was out of the country.'

She ran into his arms, hugging him about the waist. 'I'm so glad you came back. I've missed you so much the last couple of days.'

'And now I have to go away again. I could be away weeks.'

'Weeks! Oh no, Dominic, I couldn't bear it! I—I love you.'

She raised frightened eyes at the enormity of her declaration, searching his shuttered features for some sign of reaction to her words. If anything he looked even more forbidding than usual, his mouth rigid.

'What the hell did you say that for?' he rasped.

'Because it's true.'

He gave a harsh laugh. 'It's true that until two days ago you were vowing vengeance on me for stopping your marriage to Roger Young. That's the truth, Alex, not this crush you have on me.'

She shook her head. 'It isn't a crush, Dominic. I think I've always loved you, although I didn't realise it. I love you, Dominic. I do!' she cried at his scathing look.

'How can I prove it to you?'

'There is no proof of love,' he snapped. 'Only time is proof, and you haven't had time to know how you feel. Neither have I, for that matter.'

'Then you—you do feel something for me?' she asked tentatively.

He moved impatiently. 'I suppose I must do—I came back to say goodbye to you. I've never done that with any woman before.'

'Except Marianne.'

'Not always Marianne either. She was always hysterical about my going away, so in the end I didn't even bother to tell her.'

'That must have been even worse than knowing,' she shuddered. 'I would hate it.'

'Maybe it was worse; Marianne seemed to think so. The scenes she caused were unbearable, though. In the end I just stopped going home at all.'

Alexandra licked her lips. 'And am I—am I causing one of those scenes now?'

'You're building up to it,' he acknowledged grimly.

'I'm sorry, I—I don't mean to. If you'll just kiss me I'll let you go without another word.' Even if she desperately wanted to plead with him to be careful. She wouldn't become another Marianne, another clinging vine around his neck. If she was to stay in his life at all it would have to be on his terms.

'I've already told you I can't do that,' he said tersely.

'Because you'll know how you feel about me.'

'Yes.'

'Well, I want you to know,' she said determinedly. 'I want you to know, Dominic.'

Once again she moved into his arms and this time he didn't remain unresponsive, his mouth claiming hers with all the expertise she had known him capable of. His arms strained her to the hardness of his body as his lips teased hers apart to deepen the intimacy of the caress.

Nothing that had gone before had prepared her for this, for the dizziness and breathless pleasure. She could feel his pulsating hardness against her, her own body quivering with feeling, her hands enmeshed in the thickness of his hair, in no way wanting him to be gentle with her.

Dominic pulled back to draw a ragged breath. 'I knew I shouldn't have done this,' he muttered. 'It hasn't made things any easier.'

'It wasn't meant to,' she told him huskily, raising her lips for further kisses.

'You temptress!' he moaned against her parted lips.

He swung her up into his arms, laying her gently, almost reverently down on to the blue coverlet. He swiftly moved to her side, bending his head to trail his tongue along her jawbone and to the corner of her mouth as she turned to receive his kiss.

He held her immobile as he plundered her mouth, his thumbs moving rhythmically against the pulse in her throat. He moved to caress her throat with his fire-giving mouth, and Alexandra gasped at the pleasure and pain of the gently biting caresses he placed down the column of her throat and along her bare shoulders.

Dominic was shaking with the effort it took him to hold on to his self-control, his hands running down the length of her body, lingering momentarily on her taut breasts. 'This has to stop!' he said almost angrily, trying to pull out of her arms.

'Not yet, Dominic,' she clung to him. 'Stay with me a little longer.'

'Oh, Alex!' he groaned. 'I can't. I should have left fifteen minutes ago.'

'You couldn't go without knowing how I feel about you.'

'How you *think* you feel,' he corrected, this time

forcing her to release her hold on him. 'Leave it for now, Alex. We can talk when I get back.'

She sat up on the bed as he stood up, smoothing his hair with shaking hands. 'You won't have forgotten me when you come back?'

He gave her a hard look. 'Hardly.'

She blushed. 'You know what I mean.'

'Yes, I—' he broke off at a discreet knock sounded on the door. 'Come in,' he called.

Charles entered, his eyes flickering over Alexandra before coming to rest on his employer. 'The driver of the car you came in, sir, he says that if you don't leave soon you'll miss your flight.'

'Hell, yes!' Dominic ran a rough hand through his already tousled hair. 'Tell him I'll be there in five minutes, Charles.'

'Yes, sir.' He retreated stiffly out of the room.

'Your Charles doesn't approve of me,' Alexandra giggled.

'I'm not sure I do. You're shameless, coming to my room like this.'

She moved to stand in front of him, reaching up to kiss his chin. 'Absolutely,' she grinned at him. 'You make me feel like that.'

'Not now, Alex,' he moved away tersely. 'You heard Charles, I have to leave. I can't stay here any longer, I've wasted too much time already.' He picked up the case and the folder, leaving the room as hurriedly as he had entered it.

Alexandra ran after him. 'You'll let me know when you get back?' she pleaded. 'Trevor's making me move back to the house tomorrow,' she explained, 'so I won't be here when you return.'

'He's making you move out to protect you from me,' Dominic said bitterly. 'Taking you away from here won't protect you.'

'I hope not,' she said happily.

He shook his head. 'You're too much for me, Alex. I need this time away from you to look at this rationally.'

'You can't think of love as a rational thing,' she denied, running to keep up with his long strides.

'I never said anything about loving you!' he snapped harshly. 'I've never mentioned that word to you.'

'No,' she agreed slowly. 'But I mentioned it to you—and don't forget it.'

They had reached the front door by now. 'I won't forget. Now go back to your guests.'

Alexandra looked guilty. 'I'm sorry about all these people being here. There weren't supposed to be so many, but you know what it's like—you invite a few people and they all invite someone else along.' She knew she was babbling, but she didn't want him to leave.

'You can have who you like here, I don't care—as long as it isn't Young. I could cheerfully have wrung your neck last night when you said he was here with you.'

'He left soon after Trevor arrived. He's with someone else tonight.'

Dominic bent to kiss her roughly on the lips. 'Well, so are you, so don't judge him. I'll call you when I get back,' he added. 'Goodbye, Alex.'

She didn't even have time to answer him before he closed the door behind him. By the time she had wrenched open the door only the bright tail-lights of the car were visible. She stood miserably outside, watching until the lights completely disappeared.

'Where did you disappear to?' John met her in the hallway. 'You've been gone for ages.'

'I—er——' she looked at him dazedly. 'Dominic came home, I had to speak to him.'

He raised dark eyebrows. 'You mean Dominic Tempest was here and you didn't tell us? I would have loved to meet him, we all would.'

'He was in a hurry,' she said vaguely, still with Dominic. She mentally shook herself, longing to just go to her room and think of Dominic. But she couldn't, she had guests, and besides, she would have all the time she needed for thinking during the next few days. She had nothing else to do. 'How is the party going?' she asked brightly.

'Great, but we're all missing you.'

'Well, I'm back now. Let's go back in and enjoy ourselves.'

She gave a very good impression of it the next couple of hours, but in reality she was relieved when the last of them left. It had to be John, of course, he had been making mild passes at her all evening. She was finding it more and more difficult to hold him off without angering him.

'So you won't come to the party with me Saturday night?' he asked for the fifth time.

Alexandra sighed, just wanting to be alone. 'I don't have the time, John. I have my sister to look after when she gets home.'

'You have time to go to a party,' he insisted.

'No. No, I don't. It's late, John, and I——' she put up a hand to her throbbing temple. 'I have a headache. It must have been the music—and the wine,' she added ruefully.

He swayed towards her. 'Come with me on Saturday. I've been trying to date you for months now, you know that, but Roger got in before me,' his words were slightly slurred. 'But he's out of the picture now.'

'I've explained my reasons, John.' Alexandra was beginning to feel impatient now, as she gently manoeuvred him towards the door.

'You've explained *a* reason.' He wouldn't be moved. 'We've always got on together, haven't we?'

'Yes, we have. But I—I'm not in the mood for another

party.' Her voice was rising shrilly.

'Not with me, hmm? I'm beginning to think there was some truth in what Roger had to say,' he said nastily.

'What did he say?'

'Just that you and Dominic Tempest were——'

'Stop!' She didn't want to hear any more, knowing full well what Roger had had to say. 'Dominic and I are not and never have been lovers. Now who do you want to believe? Me, or Roger who's obviously feeling as if I've wronged him in some way?'

'I want to believe you,' John gave a lopsided grin, 'but I'll need proof.'

'P—proof?'

'Mm,' he pulled her roughly against him. 'Like this,' and he bent his head to claim possession of her lips.

Alexandra squirmed to avoid him. 'Stop it, John! You've drunk too much this evening.' She was panting with the effort it took her to hold off the bulkier and much stronger John. 'Will you stop it!' she pleaded desperately, finding it more and more difficult to avoid his searching mouth.

'No, I——'

'Is there anything wrong, Miss Paige?' Charles stood in the doorway behind them.

She sighed her relief, smiling gratefully at the butler. 'No, nothing, Charles. I was just seeing Mr Davies out.'

'Don't worry, I'm going,' John sneered. 'I don't need any more convincing, not when the man puts a guard over you. Roger was right, you are involved with Tempest.'

'You're being ridiculous,' she snapped.

'No, I'm not. People like Roger and me aren't good enough for you now, not when someone as famous as Dominic Tempest shows an interest. Don't worry, Charles,' John added insolently as the butler took a step towards him. 'I'm just leaving.'

'I think that would be as well, sir,' the butler agreed stiffly.

'Don't bother to show me out, I know the way.' John slammed out of the front door.

Alexandra looked at the butler shyly. 'Thank you for your help. I don't know what I would have done without you. I'm afraid Mr Davies had too much to drink.'

'Yes, miss. If you'll excuse me,' and Charles turned away.

'Oh, Charles, I—I shall be moving back to my sister's house tomorrow.'

He nodded. 'Young Mr Tempest did inform me of that earlier. Do you wish anything else tonight, miss?'

'Er—no, thank you. Goodnight, Charles.'

'Goodnight, Miss Paige.'

Alexandra tidied up the lounge before going up to her room. 'Young' Mr Tempest, Charles had called Trevor, and she supposed he was, but Dominic certainly didn't seem old to her. Tonight they had passed the point of antagonists, and now she had to wait and see how he felt about her when he returned. But whatever he felt for her she knew she would never dislike him again.

Perhaps her dislike of him had always been a shield over what she had secretly felt for him, she hadn't disliked him at all until—— But that wasn't important now, her shield was well and truly down and she didn't think it would be up again.

But Dominic had flown away into danger, unable to tell her where he was going. And she had no way of knowing when he would be back, *if* he would be back. She knew that the filming and research of his current affairs programme often involved danger, wars and revolutions being dangerous even to the uninvolved press.

Dominic had once been just a reporter, until his flair for getting the right stories at the right time and his

natural ability to keep digging until he found the truth
had all been rewarded by his own weekly television programme.

But he was a popular man in himself, his sun-bleached
blond hair and steely grey eyes earning him the adora-
tion of many women. She knew for a fact that he received hundreds of letters from these women every week,
and she now felt a jealousy towards them that made her
angry.

It was a futile anger with no reason to it; Dominic was
unlikely to meet any of these women. But there was still
Sabrina Gilbert, the woman he admitted was his mistress. But surely he wouldn't see her now, not when he
felt this attraction for her? She realised it was still a
possibility. Dominic spoke quite freely of his need for a
sexual relationship, and she didn't think she could pro-
vide that.

She had been brought up with too much morality to
enter into an affair with him, even if she was in love
with him. How would Dominic react to that? He
wouldn't like it, and it could mean his affair with
Sabrina Gilbert could continue. Dominic wasn't accustomed to denying himself.

Alexandra turned over restlessly in her bed. She had
no guarantee that he would even remember tonight's
conversation when he returned, no guarantee that he
would *want* to remember it. Well, she did, and she would
make sure he did too.

Trevor hadn't managed to arrange Gail's discharge from
the hospital the next day, his colleagues requiring her to
stay in until Saturday to make sure her condition was
stabilised. He had managed to extract a promise from
them that if everything was all right she could come
home to his and her sister's care then.

It seemed strange to be in the house on her own having

returned from visiting Gail at eight-thirty, Trevor staying on until his turn of duty had finished at nine-thirty.

Watch the programme, Dominic had said, and so she
did, her heart in her mouth as she realised it was a
revolution in one of the African states that had caused his
hurried departure of yesterday.

There was shooting going on all around him as he
continued his report, the programme obviously put
together in the London studio as flashbacks of the brew-
ing trouble were interspersed with his commentary.

Alexandra didn't know whether to laugh or cry at
being able to see him like this, aware all the time of the
distance between them and the sound of gunfire that
could be constantly heard in the background.

The trouble out there looked very serious, although
Alexandra found herself looking at Dominic rather than
listening to what was being said. How handsome he
was, how vital to her very existence. But he would be
back soon, the story had been covered now and it was
really too dangerous to stay on any longer than was
necessary. He could even be on his way back to her
right now.

This brought a smile to her lips and she stood up to
turn off the television, her hand arrested in the action
at what the newscaster had to say.

'News has just come in that shortly after these films
were flown out to us Dominic Tempest and his film
crew were taken hostage by the revolutionaries.' Alexandra sank back into her chair, intent on the man's every
word. 'We are told that the television company have
been asked for a ransom, but the amount has not been
disclosed. We will keep you informed about any further
developments. This is the end of this newsflash.'

Alexandra still sat in the chair, dazed with reaction.
This couldn't be happening, things like this didn't
happen to real people. At least, not to her. But they did

happen to people like Dominic! She didn't know if she would be able to accept it. But first he had to get out of the mess he was in! She couldn't bear it if anything happened to him.

She was jolted out of her stupor by the arrival of Trevor. He came quietly into the room, moving forward to switch off the television. He looked down at her for several minutes.

Tears filled her eyes, her face crumpling. 'Oh, Trevor, what are we going to do!'

He took her into his arms. 'There's nothing we can do but wait. I had no idea they were going to give that information out on the television or I would have tried to warn you.'

Alexandra pulled back, her eyes wide. 'You mean you knew? You knew Dominic was in danger?' Her disbelief was obvious.

Trevor moved away impatiently. 'The studio called me late this afternoon,' he confirmed.

Two angry spots appeared on her otherwise pale cheeks. 'Then why didn't you say so? You had no right to keep something like that to yourself!'

'I had every right!' he snapped tautly. 'I have a wife in hospital who would only need a shock like this to start having the baby three weeks early, and I also have a sister-in-law who imagines herself in love with my brother. What was I supposed to do,' he continued, 'tell you and hope you wouldn't tell Gail about it? I know you, Alexandra, you can't keep anything from Gail. And I will not have her worried! You understand?'

'I understand,' she accepted quietly, feeling suitably chastened. Unlike Dominic, Trevor was an even-tempered, easygoing sort of man, and it took a lot to make him angry. She had managed to do it quite easily, so she knew how deeply affected he was by his brother's disappearance. 'I'm sorry, Trevor, I wasn't thinking. I should have realised how *you* would feel, not just thought of myself.'

'It's all right, Alexandra,' he sighed. 'I realise that at the moment your feelings are too deeply involved for you to be able to see things clearly, but I did what I thought was best. I didn't think either you or Gail knowing would benefit anyone. They should have warned me the news was going to be announced after the programme. Thank God Gail doesn't have a television in her room.'

'But what did they say when they called you? What's going to happen?'

Trevor shrugged wearily. 'Exactly what they told you. Money has been asked for and it's being considered.'

'Being considered!' she repeated angrily. 'What is there to consider? Dominic is in trouble, it's their duty to help him.'

He shook his head. 'Not really. He knows the risks involved every time he goes on one of these jobs.'

'But they—they can't just leave him there,' she choked, her voice breaking emotionally.

'They don't intend to. They're doing all they can.'

'Yes, but——'

'Stop it, Alexandra,' he said wearily. 'Everything that can be done is being done. They said they'd call me if they heard anything else and so far I've heard nothing. There's been no telephone calls for me here?'

'None.'

'Then they can't have heard anything.'

Alexandra ran her hands down her levi-clad legs. 'Dominic was here last night.'

Trevor looked at her sharply. 'Last night?'

She took a deep breath. 'Yes. He—he had some papers to pick up before he left.'

'Was that all?' he asked shrewdly.

'Yes. No! I—I don't know.' She licked her lips.

'Everything between us is confused.'

'But there *is* something between you?'

'I think so. I *hope* so.'

'Something else you'll have to keep from Gail.' Trevor smiled. 'That might be as much of a shock to her as his being taken hostage. We've both got used to you hating the sight of him.'

'I've changed my mind,' she explained.

'Drastically, by the look of things,' he said dryly. 'And rather suddenly too. If—when Dominic gets back, give yourself time to see if these feelings are genuine or just an infatuation.'

'You said *if* Dominic gets back,' she looked at him worriedly. 'Do you have any doubts about it?'

'Of course not, why should I? We'll hear from the studio tomorrow, you'll see.'

But they didn't, and by late afternoon Alexandra was almost a nervous wreck. She decided to telephone the studio herself, only to be told that they weren't giving any information about Dominic Tempest and his team.

'But I'm his sister-in-law,' she insisted desperately.

The telephonist sighed. 'You must be the twentieth one today.'

'But I really am,' Alexandra said shrilly.

'That's what they all said.'

'My sister Gail is married to Dominic's brother Trevor.'

'Well, you have all the names right,' the girl said tolerably, 'so you must be quite a fan, but I'm afraid I still can't tell you anything,' and she put the phone down.

Trevor had found out little more when he came home, only that negotiations were going ahead. They didn't know when and they didn't know where the exchange would be made, and that was all they would tell him.

The hardest thing was trying to keep it from Gail,

trying to keep up a happy front and pretend that Dominic was just on a routine trip abroad. This proved difficult while Gail was in hospital, but when she was allowed home on the Saturday, with no news of Dominic, the situation became impossible.

Television and radio were banned completely, except when out of sight and earshot of Gail, and it was always a fight between Alexandra and Trevor to see who could get to the telephone first. Luckily Gail put their strange behaviour down to the fact that she had been told to rest and they didn't want her disturbed.

She did notice Alexandra's wan appearance and the dark circles under her eyes, but she put this down to her argument with Roger. It had been necessary to tell Gail of her parting from Roger, although she hadn't gone too deeply into the reasons and she hadn't explained that it was a permanent thing. But Roger was far from being the reason she couldn't eat or sleep; worry over Dominic was doing that.

It was almost a week after that fateful television programme that they heard any news. Dominic and his team were safe, and would be flown home some time during the next two days. As far as anyone knew they had not been hurt in any way.

'I'm going up to London to wait for him,' Alexandra told Trevor when he related the news to her.

'That isn't possible, Alexandra,' he said instantly. 'It could be any time during the next couple of days, and you still have Gail to care for. Besides, he'll probably be surrounded by the press for hours after he gets back, plenty of time for you to drive up to London if he wants you to.'

'If he wants me to ...' she repeated dully. 'Do you think he may not?'

He shrugged, sighing deeply. 'There's always that possibility.'

'But he——' She stopped, remembering the way Dominic had snapped when she had told him she loved him, and the way he had made it plain to her that he had never mentioned loving her. 'All right,' she agreed grudgingly. 'I'll stay here until I know what he wants.'

And so it was that she had to witness Dominic's arrival back into the country on a news bulletin at ten-thirty at night, a long time after Gail had fallen asleep. Dominic looked just as vital and attractive as ever, much more sun-tanned and very tired, but at least he was alive.

Alexandra feasted her eyes on him as he got off the plane and walked purposefully across the tarmac, watching the easy arrogance with which he carried himself, almost as if he had just returned from a holiday.

But the photographers crowding around him as he entered the airport lounge were proof that this wasn't the case, although Dominic shunned all their questions, avidly searching the crowd as if for someone special.

Alexandra gasped as she saw the someone special run into his arms. Sabrina Gilbert! And she was being thoroughly kissed by Dominic!

CHAPTER SIX

ALEXANDRA waited two days for some word from Dominic, two days during which she became more agitated than ever. Why didn't he come home, call her, *anything*?

Finally she gave up any idea of him remembering the night he had flown out of the country, any idea of her love meaning anything to him. He was probably much too involved with the lovely Sabrina Gilbert to give what he called her 'infatuation' another thought.

But she had seemed to mean something to him that night, had felt his reaction to the closeness of her body, known that he desired her, and she hadn't been afraid of that feeling.

He had telephoned Trevor, she knew that, had even spoken to Gail, but she had heard nothing from him herself. And so when John telephoned her and asked her to go out with him on Thursday evening she felt no hesitation about accepting. Besides, she needed to get out of the house for a while, and Trevor was at home tonight.

John called for her at the house, driving her over to the pub they had decided to go to. 'I'm very sorry about the other night,' he said sheepishly. 'I guess I overstepped the line. I was very insulting.'

She smiled. 'It doesn't matter. I think we'd all had too much to drink.' Especially her, if the way she had acted with Dominic was anything to go by.

'Maybe *I* had, but that didn't give me the right to be rude. I see Mr Tempest got back.' He took a sip of his beer.

'Yes,' Alexandra said abruptly, sipping the lemonade and lime she had opted for.

'A worrying time for you all,' he continued thoughtfully.

'For Trevor,' she acknowledged, glancing about them disinterestedly. 'I've never been here before, it's quite nice.'

'Not bad,' he agreed tersely. 'But weren't you worried about him? I thought you and he——'

'No!' she snapped. 'I told you there was nothing in what Roger had said. Would I be here with you now if there was anything between Dominic and myself?'

'I suppose not.' He grinned. 'And you and Roger are definitely finished?'

'Definitely. Do you have to look so happy about it?' she demanded crossly.

'Why not? It leaves the way clear for me.'

She laughed at his honesty. 'I suppose I ought to feel complimented.'

John moved along the bench seat to sit closer to her. 'Of course you did. Aren't I every young girl's dream, tall, dark and handsome?'

'Well ... you pass on two of those,' she teased.

'I won't ask which two,' he sighed. 'I can guess.' His attention became fixed on something behind her. 'Don't look now, but your boy-friend has just come in.'

Dominic! But of course it wasn't, he was still in London. Then it had to be Roger. 'He isn't my boy-friend any more,' she deliberately kept her back turned.

'Perhaps that's as well, he's with Janey again. You might as well know they've been together a lot this last week.'

'Roger is at liberty to see who he wants. It doesn't bother me in the slightest.' And it didn't, which just proved how deeply her feelings had been involved.

Nothing could equal the pain of seeing Dominic kissing that woman.

John pursed his lips. 'I hope not, because they're coming over.'

Alexander met the insolence in Roger's eyes and the challenge in Janey's both with equal coolness, unaffected by the sight of Roger's arm about his new girl-friend's shoulders. She hadn't felt any emotion at all the last couple of days, just a numb feeling that wouldn't seem to go.

'Do you mind if we join you?' Roger asked curtly.

John looked sharply at Alexandra and then back to the standing couple. 'Please yourselves.'

Janey sat down next to Alexandra and Roger had perforce to take the seat next to John. Janey smiled at her. 'Roger and I have just been to the cinema,' she announced triumphantly.

'Good film?' Alexandra asked politely, refusing to be drawn by the other girl.

'Very.' Janey put her hand on Roger's arm in a possessive gesture before looking back at Alexandra. 'You weren't at the party on Saturday.'

'No. My sister came out of hospital on that day. I've been taking care of her.'

'Gail's home?' Roger spoke to her for the first time.

'Yes,' she answered softly.

'Is everything all right now?'

She smiled at him, wishing with all her heart that she could forget Dominic and feel the jealousy she should at Roger being with another girl. 'As long as she rests.'

'I don't suppose Tempest's disappearance helped.' He couldn't keep the sneer out of his voice, evidence of his bitterness.

'Gail wasn't told until we knew he was all right,' she said stiffly.

Janey frowned. 'I gather you mean Dominic Tempest?

It would have been interesting to see tonight's programme.'

'Tonight's?' Alexandra echoed sharply.

'Mm,' Janey sipped her lager. 'It was to be a follow-up to last week's programme, all about being taken hostage and everything.'

Alexandra was very pale. 'I didn't know that.'

Janey's eyes were mischievously malicious. 'I'm surprised he didn't tell you. After all, Roger says he's your——'

'Janey!' Roger squeezed her arm painfully. 'That's enough!' he snapped.

She looked at him defiantly. 'But you did say——'

Alexandra stood up noisily. 'Excuse me, I—I have a headache.' She gave a vague smile in their direction before running across the room.

Dominic had been on television this evening and she had missed him. She hadn't for one moment imagined he would carry on and do a programme after what he had been through the past week. She should have known better, should have realised that his job was the most important thing to him.

Roger caught up with her at the door, swinging her round to face him. 'I'm sorry about that, Alexandra. Believe me when I say I wouldn't like to cause you any more pain—you look as if you've suffered enough already.'

She smiled wanly. 'Thank you.'

'Loving someone who doesn't love you can be a hard thing to bear,' he added softly. 'I should know.'

She looked deeply into his clouded brown eyes and touched his hand briefly. 'I'm sorry, Roger,' she bit her lip. 'I've made a mess of everything.'

'It doesn't have to be this way,' he said almost eagerly. 'I would take you back now if you just said the word.'

And she would have loved to be able to say that

word, but there would be no point to it. She had grown out of her girlish love for Roger and into the painful love of a woman for a man she couldn't have.

John came to her side. 'Are you ready to leave now, Alexandra?'

Roger looked at her pleadingly. 'Alexandra?'

She sighed. 'I'm sorry, Roger, I really am. And yes, I'm ready to go home, John.' She touched Roger's arm. 'Goodnight,' she said softly.

'Goodnight,' he echoed dully.

'Janey's a bitch,' said John once they were on their way back to her home. 'She was being deliberately provocative.'

Alexandra smiled in the darkness. 'She was fighting for the man she wants.'

'I think she lost that round,' he said grimly. 'Roger was furious with her for baiting you like that.'

'Janey obviously lives by the rule that all's fair in love and war.'

'Mm, well, I think she now knows that Roger still loves you, so her tactics didn't pay off.'

'Rubbish,' she told him primly. 'Roger and I are finished, he knows that.'

He gave a short laugh. 'It doesn't stop him loving you.'

Her hands moved jerkily. 'I don't want to talk about it any more.' She saw they were fast approaching her home. 'Thank you for taking me out this evening. I've——'

'Don't say you've enjoyed yourself!' he interrupted abruptly. 'We both know you haven't. I should have taken you somewhere out of the area, somewhere where we wouldn't be likely to run into Roger.'

It hadn't been Roger who had ruined her evening, it had been the talk of Dominic. Seeing him on the television might have been seeing him second-hand, but at least it would have been seeing him.

'It isn't important, John,' she told him gently. 'I——'

She broke off as she saw the car parked in the drive-way. Dominic's car! Dominic was here visiting Trevor and Gail. He must have driven here straight after the broadcasting of his programme—and she had almost missed him!

She could hardly wait for the car to stop before opening the door and beginning to scramble out. 'Thank you, John,' she said hurriedly. 'I'll see you again soon.'

'When?' He too got out of the car.

She was impatient to be gone. 'I—I'm not sure. I—Why don't you call me?'

'Does that car happen to belong to Dominic Tempest?' he asked shrewdly.

'Yes.' She could see no point in prevaricating.

'Okay,' he sighed, 'I'll call you.'

Alexandra let herself into the house, throwing her jacket and handbag on to the hall table before entering the lounge where a murmur of voices could be heard. Her eyes went straight to Dominic as he sat sprawled in one of the armchairs, feasting her eyes on him.

The television of his arrival back into this country had been slightly deceptive about his condition. He looked very, very tired and he had lost about a stone in weight, in fact he didn't look at all well. Alexandra's heart went out to him, but the coolness of his steely grey eyes did not encourage her in any way.

Gail lay on the sofa, obviously carried there by her husband on this special occasion of Dominic's visit. 'Did you have a nice evening?' she asked her young sister.

Alexandra couldn't take her eyes off Dominic, although if anything his expression was even more remote. 'Yes, thank you,' she answered breathlessly, her mind not really on what was being said.

'Perhaps you would like to make some coffee,' Gail

suggested. 'I think we could all do with a cup.'

Trevor stood up. 'Any coffee you have can be drunk in bed. You've been up quite enough for one day.' He swung her up into his arms. 'And no arguments,' he warned as she made to protest. 'You'll do as you're told or you'll go straight back into hospital.'

'Yes, Trevor,' she smiled up at him. 'What a father you're going to make!'

Dominic stood up. 'No coffee for me either,' he said abruptly. 'I only called round briefly to see that Gail was all right.'

'Me?' Gail scoffed. '*I* didn't get myself taken hostage. Having a baby is quite tame compared to that!'

'There was absolutely no danger involved to me or anyone else. These people just wanted the money to buy more arms,' he added dryly. 'It would have caused too much of an incident if they'd harmed us in any way. They want support for their cause, not bad publicity.'

'Well, I'm just glad you're safe, although it was very naughty of these two to keep it from me.' Gail yawned tiredly. 'I must be more tired than I realised.'

'Bed for you, young lady,' her husband said sternly. 'You've been up far too long as it is. No doubt you'll see Dominic tomorrow.'

'I love it when he's so domineering,' she giggled.

Dominic nodded curtly to them all and left. Alexandra was too stunned at first to realise he had actually gone, but once she did realise she hurried after him, catching up with him just as he was unlocking his car door.

'Dominic,' she said breathlessly.

He looked at her with narrowed eyes. 'Yes?'

'Are you really all right?' Now that she was here she didn't know what to say.

'Really,' he said mockingly. 'You'd better get in, they'll be wondering where you are.'

'Dominic, I—you——' she moved from one foot to

the other. 'I've been waiting to hear from you.'

'Why?' he asked coldly.

Her eyes widened. 'Why? Because of what happened between us, because I've been worried to death about you. Isn't that reason enough?'

'Nothing happened between us, Alexandra,' he said with a sigh. 'I told you at the time not to read too much into it.'

She gasped. 'You can't mean that! You kissed me, you came back to say goodbye to me,' she added desperately.

'I've kissed hundreds of girls,' he dismissed. 'As for saying goodbye to you, you were there, that's all.'

'I don't believe you. You said——'

'I said a lot of things,' he interrupted harshly. 'That doesn't mean you had to take them seriously.'

'So Sabrina Gilbert meeting you at the airport *did* mean something,' she choked. 'I hoped——' she shook her head, the ready tears gathering in her deep blue eyes. 'It doesn't matter. I should have realised your cruel sense of humour would find something like this amusing.'

Dominic's face was harsh in the moonlight. 'You don't know the meaning of the word cruel. And of course Sabrina meeting me meant something. She cared enough to be there.'

'So did I! But——'

'There's always a but, Alexandra,' he snapped. 'Get inside and go to bed, there's a good girl.'

'Don't talk to me as if I'm a child! I'm no longer a schoolgirl, you know. I go to college.'

'So Trevor informed me.'

'Why should he tell you that?' she asked sharply.

'Probably so that I could stop paying your school fees,' he said abruptly.

'You—you paid for my schooling?'

'Some of it,' he acknowledged.

All these years and she had never known. No wonder he had scoffed at her when she had told him to stop interfering in her life! 'I didn't know,' she whispered dazedly.

'Why should you?' Dominic swung into the driving seat. 'It didn't concern you.'

'Didn't concern me!' she repeated shrilly. 'Of course it concerned me. I don't like being beholden to you for anything.'

His teeth gleamed whitely in the moonlight. 'It didn't take you long to get back to the spitting wildcat I'm used to. I think I prefer it.'

'Perhaps that's as well,' she said bitterly. 'I doubt I'll ever make a fool of myself like this again. You teach a hard lesson, Mr Tempest, but you teach it well. I'll concede defeat to Miss Gilbert and women like her.'

'You do that.' He started the car engine. 'Go back to your dolls, Alexandra.'

'Why, you——'

'Let me know when you want any more lessons on growing up,' his grey eyes mocked her.

'You've already taught me one I won't forget.' She turned on her heel. 'Goodbye.'

'Goodnight, Alex,' he said softly.

That name—how dared he call her that name! With a sob Alexandra ran into the house, vaguely conscious of the roar of the car engine as he accelerated away. He was cruel, very cruel—and she still loved him!

Trevor found her in the kitchen preparing the coffee Gail had asked for, the tears streaming down her face. 'It will be ready in a minute,' she sniffed, her head averted.

'You went after Dominic.' It was a statement, not a question.

'Yes—and I wish I hadn't.'

'I did warn you, Alexandra,' he said gently. 'I know

Dom of old, and Marianne did scar him pretty badly.'

'Does that mean every other female has to pay for it?' she demanded angrily. 'He's cold and ruthless and he— he deliberately let me believe—let me believe——'

Trevor shook his head. 'I'm sure he did no such thing. Dom has never needed to go to that extreme. On the contrary, women have always been falling over themselves to go out with him. I remember I used to envy him a lot when I was younger.'

Alexandra's blue eyes flashed. 'You have nothing to envy him for,' she said vehemently.

He grinned. 'I know that now, but at the time ... But I wouldn't change one minute of my time with Gail for all of his social whirl.'

'His women, you mean,' she snapped.

'If you like,' Trevor nodded. 'You can't blame him for taking advantage of his attraction.'

She could if he used her as one of his experiments! 'Dominic said—your brother said that he—that he paid for my schooling.'

Trevor turned away. 'When did he tell you that?'

Alexandra bit her top lip. 'Just now.'

'You must have given him great provocation,' he looked at her thoughtfully. 'I gather you had quite an argument.'

'Yes. Is it true, Trevor? Did he pay for me to go to boarding-school?'

He sighed. 'Yes.'

'But why? I didn't need to go to a private school, I could have gone to the local daily school like most of the other kids in the area.'

'Dom didn't want that. He——'

'It had nothing to do with him! If I'd known he had a hand in it I would have refused to go to the school!'

Trevor smiled. 'I think he knew that, that's why he made Gail and me promise not to tell you. I suppose that now you've left he didn't see the need to keep it a secret any longer.'

Or else he had just wanted to hurt her some more! Well, he had done that; she only hoped he left her alone now. 'Probably. Here,' she handed him a cup of the cooling coffee, 'take this to Gail before it's undrinkable.'

Trevor gently touched her flushed cheeks. 'Don't fret about Dom. He may have been a little harsh on you tonight, but he's been through a lot this past week. I couldn't even let Gail watch the programme in case she saw just how rough things were for him.'

'But he—said there was never any danger.'

'He lied for Gail's sake. We had a long conversation on the telephone the night he got back, and I can assure you he didn't get to look the way he does tonight by sleeping on a feather bed and eating three-course meals.'

'I didn't realise,' she said slowly.

'Think about it, chicken,' he advised softly. 'And don't judge his behaviour tonight too harshly.'

Alexandra made her way to her bedroom, her thoughts solely on Dominic. Perhaps she was judging him too harshly, he had been through a lot, never knowing from one minute to the next whether he was going to live or die. But he had been deliberately cruel to her, made her feel like a juvenile with a crush on an older man. But perhaps that was what she seemed to him. She certainly wasn't acting very grown-up.

She hadn't considered anything but the fact that Dominic hadn't been in contact with her. It would have been just as easy for her to contact him. And tonight when he had come here she had been out with another man, hardly the act of a woman who was supposed to be in love with him.

But there was no supposition about it; she did love him, and she had to tell him so—even if he didn't want to hear it. If she told him and he still rebuffed her she would at least know where she stood.

Her mind made up, there seemed only one course of action. She had to go and see Dominic—and see him now. She wouldn't be able to sleep until she had spoken to him and so she might as well go over there as soon as she was sure Trevor and Gail were asleep.

It was almost one o'clock in the morning before she considered it safe. She crept quietly out of her bedroom and made her way down the stairs, noticing for the first time the two creaky steps half way down. She had never noticed them before, but then she had never tried to sneak out of the house unheard before either.

She had almost reached the back door when she realised she was no longer alone. Turning slowly, she saw a huge dark figure in the open doorway. Her eyes opened wide with fear as she imagined that on the one night she had tried to get out of the house undetected a burglar should come to call.

The light beside the kitchen door was flicked on and she blinked rapidly in the sudden glare. 'Trevor!' she breathed his name softly, her relief evident. 'You gave me a scare!'

He closed the door softly behind him. 'I should damn well think so,' he snapped angrily. 'Just what do you think you're up to?'

'How did you hear me?' She ignored his question, frantically searching in her mind for a good excuse for being down here. 'I thought I'd been so quiet.'

'You were,' he whispered. 'But Gail is a light sleeper at the moment. She thought she heard burglars.'

She gave a soft laugh. 'And I thought you were one!'

He gave her an impatient look, the usually even-tempered Trevor truly angry. 'I asked you what you were doing,' he said curtly.

'I was—I was getting a drink of water,' she told him,

realising how weak that sounded even to her own ears.

He raised his eyebrows. 'Fully dressed? You went to your room hours ago.'

'Yes,' she smiled brightly, 'but I was reading. I—I hadn't got ready for bed yet.'

'You lie very badly, Alexandra. Now tell me what you were really doing.'

'I—I was just going out for a breath of fresh air,' she lied.

'The real reason, Alexandra,' he said hardly.

'I was going to see Dominic,' she admitted miserably.

'At one o'clock in the morning?'

Her eyes were beseeching. 'I have to see him.'

'You've already seen him once this evening. Nothing has changed since then.'

'*I've* changed. I need to see him, Trevor.'

He sighed deeply. 'I know I told you to think about it, but I didn't expect your conclusions to make you take off in the dead of night. Can't it wait until morning, Alexandra?'

She shook her head obstinately, her mouth set in a stubborn line. 'I'll never sleep, so it might as well be now.'

'But *he* could be asleep. He has a lot to catch up on.'

'If he is asleep I won't disturb him.'

'Okay,' he gave in with a sigh. 'I know you in this mood, nothing will change your mind.'

'No,' she admitted.

'All right, I'll be listening for your return. But don't make too much noise getting in, and make sure you aren't too late,' he ordered firmly. 'I would hate to have to come and drag you out of Dom's arms.'

Alexandra's mouth twisted. 'I doubt that will be necessary.'

'I hope not. I'll go back upstairs now and try to persuade Gail she imagined it all.' He grimaced. 'It won't be easy. Drive carefully,' he warned.

The roads were quite deserted this time of night, this part of Hampshire not exactly teeming with night-life. Alexandra saw the odd car going in the opposite direction, but other than that it was a lonely drive over to Dominic's house.

The house was in darkness as she approached the front door, except for a single light burning in the lounge. Unless the light had been left on as a precaution against burglary it meant Dominic was still up.

She let herself in, creeping quietly through the house so as not to disturb the watchful Charles. The last thing she needed right now was the stiff politeness of the butler; she was nervous enough about being here without that.

The opening of the lounge door seemed very loud to her ears and she looked around furtively before entering the room. Only the side-lamp illuminated the room, and Dominic sat slumped in an airmchair, his eyes closed, an empty glass dangling from his fingers. His face was pale and drawn, his hair ruffled and untidy as if he had been running his fingers through its blond thickness. He looked tired, so very tired, and she hesitated about disturbing him.

Just as she had made up her mind to leave the grey eyes flickered open, pinning her to the spot. 'What are you doing here?' he shot the question at her like a whiplash.

Alexandra felt tongue-tied now she actually had the chance to speak to him, afraid of the outcome of this conversation. 'I wanted to talk to you,' she said softly.

'How did you get in?' He stood up to pour himself another drink. 'I didn't hear anyone at the door.'

'I still have the key you gave me.' She put it on a side-table. 'I didn't want to bother Charles.'

Dominic gave a humourless smile. 'I doubt he would have approved of letting you in this time of night. Does

Trevor know you're here?'

'Yes.'

'Is that the truth?' His eyes were narrowed.

Alexandra flushed. 'I don't tell lies,' she snapped.

'All women lie,' he said bitterly, downing most of the whisky in the glass in one gulp.

'Dominic!' she gasped his name.

'All right, all right,' he snapped. 'So you told Trevor you were sneaking over here, and for some reason he allowed you to come. I suppose that was mainly due to the fact that he knew he wouldn't be able to stop you,' he added dryly.

'Yes,' she admitted.

'Don't you think it's time you stopped thinking of yourself and considered other people for a change?' he demanded harshly.

'It's because I can't stop thinking about *you* that I'm here,' she choked.

He raised his eyebrows. 'Thinking of me? Why on earth should you be thinking of me?'

She looked at him with tortured eyes. 'Now that I'm actually with you I don't know.' Seeing him like this, so arrogant, so coldly withdrawn from her, she didn't know how she had dared to come here at all.

'Then perhaps you'd better leave,' said Dominic callously.

'No! I—I don't want to, not yet. I have to know how you feel about me.'

Dominic gave her an impatient look. 'We've already had this conversation once tonight.'

She shook her head. 'No, we haven't. You were cruel and unkind to me, but we didn't actually talk.'

'I thought we had,' he disagreed wearily. 'In any case, I'm too tired right now to try and placate a juvenile.'

'You see, you're doing it again!'

His eyes blazed with anger. 'Will you please leave,

Alexandra! I'm tired and I want to go to bed.'

'I'm surprised you aren't there already, you left us hours ago.'

'And would you have violated my bedroom too?' he snapped.

'I already have, once,' she reminded him softly.

He turned away. 'Leave, Alexandra!'

'Won't you call me Alex?' she invited.

'You don't like it.'

'I do when *you* call me it. Dominic, I—I wanted to come to the airport to meet you, but Trevor wouldn't let me. He said you would call me if you wanted me.'

'What the hell does he know about it?' he rasped.

'He knows everything,' she told him shyly.

'Everything?' he echoed. 'What is everything?'

'That we're attracted to each other, that you came back to the house the night you flew out of the country, that I—that I love you.' She looked at him pleadingly, begging for his understanding.

'Not that again, Alex,' he said with a sigh. 'You don't understand the meaning of the commitment of the word. Your love was so strong that tonight you were out with another man. And don't attempt to deny it, Gail was full of the fact that you seem to have got over the idea of marrying Young. Who was this one, another poor sap who thinks you're going to marry him?'

'John thinks no such thing! He——'

'John Anderson?' he queried sharply.

'Yes. Do you know him?'

Dominic shook his head. 'I know his father. He's more my generation,' he added tauntingly.

She ignored his deliberate jibe about their age difference. 'Well, I didn't know what to do. I wanted to come up to London, but as I said, Trevor wouldn't let me. And you didn't call me, so I didn't know how you would feel about my coming up there. Plus there was Sabrina

Gilbert. She met you at the airport. I saw you kissing her,' and she looked at him accusingly.

'Did you indeed?'

'Yes, I did!'

He sighed. 'I would have kissed Dracula's sister at the time. I was just glad to see a familiar face. It wasn't the face I expected to see, but it was better than nothing.'

Alexandra looked puzzled. 'But on the television you appeared to be looking for her.'

He watched her closely. 'Not for Sabrina,' he denied softly.

'Then who——' her eyes widened. '*Me?* You were looking for me?'

He poured himself another drink. 'Stupid, wasn't it? I somehow had the idea you would want to be there. When you weren't—well, it just confirmed my suspicion that you were temporarily suffering from a teenage crush. When it came to harsh reality you couldn't take the pressure.'

Alexandra put her arms about his waist from behind, her head resting on his broad back. 'That isn't true, Dominic. Oh, I'll admit that when I first heard of your being taken hostage I was completely panic-stricken. But I'll get used to it,' her hold about him tightened. 'I will, Dominic,' she said desperately. 'Really, I will!'

He released her hands from about his waist and turned to look at her, their two bodies pressed close together. He ran one hand down her fevered cheeks. 'Don't get too used to that sort of thing happening, Alex,' he warned softly. 'I'm not sure I could go through that again myself.' His body shook against her. 'I wanted so much to see you, and I didn't hear from you.' His voice was agonised.

Alexandra burrowed against him, sensing his weakening towards her. 'I thought you would come straight home, I never expected you to stay in London. Trevor said you'd be surrounded by the press and that if I meant anything to you you'd call me and I'd have plenty of time to get up to London before the press finished with you.'

Dominic bent his head to trail his lips across her creamy throat. 'My brother doesn't know everything,' he said softly, his breath caressing on her skin. 'We parted with too much uncertainty between us for me to be confident of your feelings when I returned. By telephoning you I would have been putting pressure on you I didn't feel I had the right to inflict.'

'Oh, Dominic ...' she breathed against his hair-roughened skin visible between the open neckline of his shirt. 'You're right about me, I *am* juvenile. I went out with John tonight as a salve against my injured pride, not because I really wanted to.'

'That's not so juvenile. Didn't I do that same thing with Sabrina?'

'Have you been with her the last two days?' She felt her heart would break if he said yes.

'No,' he said tautly. 'I had a programme to do. Wednesday and Thursday are the usual days for recording. I was referring to kissing her at the airport.'

'Dominic, do you—do you know how you feel about me now?' she asked tentatively.

'I know that all the time I was away I kept thinking about you, kissing you, just being with you. I also know I've never felt this way about any woman before. But whether or not it's love I have no idea. But even if it is I have no intention of marrying you.'

CHAPTER SEVEN

ALEXANDRA stiffened in his arms. 'I'm not asking you for marriage.'

'Not ever?' His hold on her arms didn't slacken as he forced her to look at him. 'Are you saying you would never ask me for marriage?'

Alexandra bit her lip, her eyes never flinching from his steely grey ones. 'Not if you don't want it,' she answered breathlessly.

His fingers bit into her tender flesh. 'You would go on for years never knowing whether the next day was going to be the day I did find the woman I want to marry, you would be my mistress with none of the security of marriage? Would you be prepared to do that, Alex?'

'There's no security even in marriage if you don't have love,' she evaded.

'That wasn't the question,' Dominic insisted grimly.

She wrenched out of his arms, glaring her resentment at him. 'Yes, I'll do that if it's what you want! I don't have any choice, do I?'

'Yes, you have a choice.' To her surprise he smiled. 'When I said I wouldn't marry you, I meant I wouldn't marry you *now*.'

Alexandra frowned. 'I don't understand you.'

Dominic sat down. 'When you asked Gail and Trevor for permission to marry Roger you'd only known him for a few months; *we've* discovered we're attracted to each other in only a matter of days.'

'Time doesn't matter,' she interrupted.

'Of course it matters,' he denied tersely. 'I dis-

approved of your marrying him because of your youth
and the fact that you hadn't been going out together
very long. Neither of those reasons is any different just
because of a change of boy-friend. I couldn't ask Gail
and Trevor to change their minds just because it's me,
that would be like admitting *we* were unsure of how we
felt.'

'You haven't told me how you feel yet, only that
you've been thinking about me.'

Dominic grinned, beckoning her over to him. 'I
would rather show you,' he drawled throatily.

She blushed profusely. 'You're embarrassing me.'

'Then come here,' he invited softly. 'If I can touch
you perhaps I won't keep staring at you.'

Alexandra looked down self-consciously. 'This
wasn't the way I wanted it to be. I wanted to be wearing a floating black creation, my hair in a sophisticated
style, everything about me sophisticated. Instead of
which I'm wearing these awful denims and this green
sun-top. I didn't think at the time, I just grabbed the
first thing I laid my hands on.' She was babbling again,
but somehow the look in his eyes had that effect on
her.

He lay slumped down in the chair. 'I wouldn't care
if you were wearing nothing—in fact I would prefer it.'
He chuckled at her embarrassment. 'If you intend being
my girl-friend you'll have to get used to remarks like
that.'

She came forward hesitantly, coming to stand in
front of his splayed legs. 'Am I going to be your girl-
friend?'

'Oh, I think so, don't you?' He put out a hand to
grasp her wrist, pulling her down into his arms. 'Somehow I don't feel tired any more.' He cupped her face
in his hands, his head moving down slowly so that his
lips claimed hers.

As soon as his lips parted hers to deepen the kiss she felt herself responding to him, her arms about his neck to hold him to her. The kiss was deep and drugging, his mouth seeming to plunder her very soul. His hands moved ceaselessly over her back, bringing her closer and closer to the hardness of his body.

But Alexandra felt none of the panic that Roger's kisses in her bedroom had evoked, knowing only pleasure in Dominic's arms. He was a master of the art of love-making but held a very tight control over his actions with her. His lips on her throat scorched where they touched, his hands on her back moulded her to him. But he made no effort to touch her in a more intimate way, even though her body cried out for it.

'Dominic,' she said tentatively.

'Mm?' He was intent on the sensitive area beneath her ear-lobe.

'Dominic, do you—do you want me?' She wriggled with pleasure as his tongue probed the sensitive cord in her throat.

'What do you think?' he growled.

'Then why——'

'That's another of the conditions,' his voice was muffled in her hair.

'C—conditions?'

'Mm. I made up my mind while I was away that if you were still set on the idea of loving me I would have to set myself a few conditions. One of them is that if we do decide to get married it won't be for six months, not until you're eighteen.'

Her dismay showed on her face. 'But that's ages!'

'Do you think I don't know that?' he groaned. 'It will seem even longer to me, I'm not accustomed to being with innocents. I'm not used to denying myself either. I've had a very varied sex-life since Marianne and I were divorced. I'm not even sure if I'll be able to stand the strain, but I'll give it a damn good try— as long as you don't try and tempt me too often. That's the other condition, nothing physical between us until we're sure of each other.'

'If you aren't—making love to me will you go to Sabrina Gilbert?' Alexandra felt it was a question she just had to ask him.

'No,' he answered abruptly. 'On Tuesday night, after I got away from the press, we went back to my apart- ment as we usually do. I'm not going to lie to you—I needed someone desperately that night. But it was no good for us. Sabrina blamed it on the trauma of the last week, but I knew that wasn't the reason. A pair of deep blue eyes kept haunting me. It was the most humiliating experience I've ever been through.'

'I'm glad,' She kissed his strong jawline.

'You're pleased that I couldn't make it as a man?'

'With another woman, yes.'

His fingers trailed along her cheek. 'How do you know I'll be able to make it with you?' he teased.

'I did offer,' she reminded him.

His arms tightened about her. 'And I would love to accept that offer, however innocently it was made. I want you like hell!'

'Oh, Dominic!' She melted against him, the dark sheen of her hair like a curtain about them.

'But it's not possible,' he said sternly. 'It's part of the conditions. We could become blinded by a physi- cal relationship. I know damn well I could lose myself in you, and I don't want our judgment to be clouded in that way. If we do marry it will be because we're genuinely in love with each other, not because we have something good going for us physically.'

'So you're testing me, testing to see if my love will last.'

'I'm testing myself too, Alex. It would be so easy to

take you to my bed right now, but that isn't the way I want it to be. I made a mess of my first marriage, I don't intend for that to happen again. I can't even believe I'm making this much of a commitment to you. I swore I would never get emotionally involved with another woman.'

'*Are* you emotionally involved with me?'

'The word love is used too casually these days. I want to be very sure before I say it to you. Let's just be satisfied with what we have for the moment and see how it goes. No talk of marriage, especially to other people. I want people to just get used to seeing us together. There will be a lot of talk, you know that?'

'I don't care.' She clung to him.

'Some of it could get malicious,' he warned. 'This is a village, Alex, and some of the women around here would just love to find a scandal in our going out together. They would have a field-day if they knew you were here now.'

'I still don't care.'

'I hope you feel the same in a couple of months. I suppose you realise I'm notorious in this area? I lure innocent females to my house and ravish them.'

Alexandra giggled. 'I'm sure most of them wanted to be ravished.'

Dominic chuckled. 'I can't believe this is you and me here like this. If it had been suggested to me I would probably have laughed at the idea.'

She frowned. 'Regretting it already?'

'I'm hoping I never will. I'm really hoping this will be for ever.'

She smoothed away the frown from between his eyes. 'I'll try to make it so.'

'Give yourself time, little one. Learn to like before you love.'

She gave him a rueful look. 'I'm afraid I've been so

busy hating you in the past that there's been no room for liking.'

'Do you remember why you started hating me? You never used to, you know.'

'Didn't I?' She made to move out of his arms, but he held her fast. 'It seems like I always did.'

'Alex,' he probed softly. 'Don't shut it out of your mind, not now. There has to be complete honesty between us. I had too many lies from Marianne to want it to happen that way again. I want to talk about it, Alex, about the day I rudely awakened you from your childhood.'

Her laugh was strained. She had put the thought out of her mind for so long now that it was still painful to remember, the day Dominic had come crashing down off the pedestal she had placed him on. 'Hardly that, Dominic,' she said lightly. 'I was fifteen at the time, high time I began to realise the facts of life.'

'So you do remember it.' He studied her deeply. 'I always thought it was the reason, but I could never be sure. There was a time when my home was almost your home, when you walked in and out of here as if I was your brother. Until the day you walked into one room too many.'

Her face was pale now. 'It was my own fault. I—I should have realised. I knew you had Julia staying here. I just didn't expect . . .'

'I didn't expect you to walk in there either. Julia walked out on me muttering all sorts of threats. I was furious with you at the time.'

'I was so shocked,' Alexandra admitted shakily. 'Maybe even then I secretly wanted it to have been me.'

'Do you mind!' he exclaimed indignantly. 'I feel like a cradle-snatcher now, let alone considering seducing a fifteen-year-old.' He gently pushed her head down on to his shoulder. 'Never mind, darling, we'll take a shower together one day and perhaps that will blot the memory of Julia and me together out of your mind.'

It was already forgotten. It had been an incident blown up out of all proportion in her mind. Dominic's latest girl-friend had been staying with him and Alexandra had walked in on them as they were stepping out of the shower together. It had been a shock to see him so intimate with another woman—and she had begun to hate him from that moment on.

She glowed now at his use of the endearment. 'I'll look forward to it.'

Dominic took a deep breath. 'I think I'd better get you home now, before I break my own rule.'

'Oh, not yet, Dominic,' she pleaded.

'Right now. Do you realise that it's almost two-thirty in the morning? You'll have Trevor out here looking for you soon.' He pushed her to her feet, standing at her side. 'And we don't want to start off on the wrong foot with him. He may be my brother, but he also has a large say in your future.'

'Not once I'm eighteen.'

'Even then. I won't marry you without their permission.'

That he was considering marrying her at all was more than she had dared to hope. 'Surely Trevor wouldn't refuse his own brother?'

Dominic smoothed back his ruffled hair. 'He knows me better than anyone, the life I've led, the women I've had, so he has all the more reason to object.'

'But you couldn't be expected not to—not to have had women. You're a very virile man.' Her eyes teased him. 'I have a very vivid picture of you in my mind as you stepped naked out of that shower. You have a beautiful body.'

His eyes had darkened almost to black. 'Come here,'

he groaned, pulling her into his arms, his body evidence of how her words had aroused him.

His kiss was savage, blotting out all of the gentleness he had treated her with earlier, and yet Alexandra loved him all the more for it. She loved the way his mouth moved demandingly on her own, the way the fierce passion between them threatened to consume them both. It was a feeling she welcomed, and her body strained against him for more intimate contact.

She shivered slightly as Dominic dispensed with the buttons on her cotton sun-top, but it was a shiver of pure delight, not one of fear, and the quivering increased as he released the single front-fastening to her bra, cupping her breasts to stroke the taut nipples to full pulsating life.

Then they were no longer standing but lying side by side on the sofa, Dominic seeming to have lost all desire to resist her. His mouth soon replaced those caressing hands, his lips and tongue making her gasp out his name in pleasure. She had never known such mindless pleasure before, never dreamt it could be like this with a man, a man one loved.

He lifted his head, his eyes glazed with passion. 'Oh God, Alex, I should have sent you home hours ago, while I still had the power to resist you.'

She caressed his nape, loving the feel of his hair through her fingers. 'I don't want you to resist me. Just go on loving me. It feels so good!'

His look was agonised. 'I know, that's what I was afraid of. I don't want any other woman, being with Sabrina proved that, and yet I could take you here and now, *revel* in you. But you can feel that, can't you, feel the way I want you.'

'Yes.'

'Oh, Alex!' His mouth claimed hers again as he pressed her back against the softness of the sofa.

Alexandra didn't notice his weight on her, aware only of the hard demand of his body against her thighs, of his own bare chest revealed by his open shirt against the nakedness of her breasts. One of his hands ran from her thigh to her breasts in slow circular movements, setting her aflame wherever he touched.

Finally he drew back with a gasp. 'If this doesn't stop in a minute I'm going to lose control completely.'

She looked up at him. 'You once told me that being old and ancient it takes more than a beautiful face and a youthful body to turn you on.'

There was a fine sheen of perspiration on his brow. 'Yes, well, perhaps I'm not as old and ancient as I thought I was. I'm almost at breaking point with you.'

'Only almost?' Now she knew what Dominic had meant when he had said she couldn't be in love with Roger if she had never been tempted to go to bed with him—she was more than tempted with Dominic, she wanted it to be a reality.

'No,' he groaned. 'I am at breaking point!'

Alexandra met the passion in his kiss with equal fervour, stripping his shirt from his shoulders, caressing his muscular back with her finger-tips. 'I love you, Dominic,' she gasped at the explosion of feeling between them, the hard thrusting of his body met by her own frantic clamouring for his possession of her,

'If you love me, Alex, then help me,' he begged. 'Please, help me!'

'But, Dominic——'

'Alex, please!' He was shaking against her.

She knew he meant it, knew she had to stop him or risk his burning anger afterwards. But it wasn't easy to dampen down her own desire, not when she had so recently discovered just how wonderful it could be.

Finally she managed to gain some control over herself, cradling Dominic to her as he visibly fought for control. His head rested on her shoulder, his breathing soon calming down to a more even tone.

'I nearly went over the edge then,' he said with a sigh, his face buried in her hair, his arm about her waist. 'Thank you for stopping me.'

She kissed his brow. 'I didn't want to.'

His hold tightened. 'I know you didn't,' he said gently. 'But it's for the best.' He stood up, pulling on his shirt. 'I'll take you home now, it's very late. Trevor will have a search party out soon.'

Alexander felt no self-consciousness as she re-arranged her own clothing. 'He knows where I am.'

Dominic grinned. 'That's why I think he might come looking for you!'

'He wouldn't.' She stood up, moving forward to kiss him softly on the lips.

'Certainly not because he trusts me,' he smiled at her.

'No,' she agreed with a laugh. 'But he trusts me.'

'Then he shouldn't,' he said gravely.

'No, but he doesn't know that. Neither did I until just now. I—er—I'm not sure I'll be able to last six months.'

Dominic moved away. 'I'll make sure you do. All right,' he added at her scathing look, 'I know that wasn't a very good example of control, but I'm prepared for you now. At least you've restored my faith in my ability to satisfy a woman. I wonder if you know just how close you came to being taken right there on that sofa.'

Alexandra blushed. 'I think I do.'

'Right, well, you'll know not to push your luck too far again.'

'You aren't saying that we can't be alone?' she asked in dismay.

His eyes deepened in colour. 'No, I'm not saying

that. I *need* to be able to kiss you, to hold you, but if I make any moves to touch you like that again you have to stop me.'

'I'm not sure if I can.'

'Just try.' He put his hand out to her. 'Come on, I'll take you home.'

'I'm not sure you should drive—you've been drinking tonight.'

'I'm stone cold sober now. Passion has a way of doing that,' he derided. 'Besides, it's late. I don't want you driving alone.'

Alexandra smiled at him shyly. 'You're very considerate all of a sudden.'

'I have to be if I'm going to keep my young girlfriend interested in me.'

'You're mocking me now,' she said crossly.

'I'm mocking myself, Alex. Shall we go out to dinner tomorrow—today?'

'That would be nice,' she answered primly.

Dominic laughed throatily, pulling her into his arms. 'Now I've upset you,' he lifted her chin to gently kiss her on the lips. 'I was only teasing, darling.'

She relaxed against him. 'Am I allowed to tell Gail and Trevor about us?'

'We don't know if there is any *us* to tell anyone about yet, but I should think that by this time Trevor has a fair idea of what's happening. They'll realise soon enough that we're going out together, that we feel something for each other, but there'll be time enough in the future to talk to them about marriage. We don't even know if it's going to happen yet.'

Alexandra frowned. 'Do you have doubts?'

'At this moment, no. But I have to be sure you can take the life I live before we make any definite plans.'

She let him drive her home, wishing that she felt more sure of his feelings for her. Even after all that had been said and done tonight Dominic still hadn't told her he loved her. But he wasn't a man who liked commitments, not after the obvious failure of his first marriage, and she would just have to be satisfied with things as they were.

He had more than proved that he was physically attracted to her, but could hold on to his self-control with her. She had his respect at least, it was a start.

As Dominic brought the car to a halt outside the house Trevor came out to meet them, dressed in his nightclothes. 'Do you realise what the time is?' he attacked his brother. 'Alexandra's been gone almost three hours,' he accused.

She got out of the car. 'Please, Trevor——'

'Let me handle this, Alex,' Dominic cut in. 'You go inside. I'll see you this evening, about eight o'clock.'

She wanted to kiss him goodnight, but Trevor looked angry enough already without that. 'All right,' she squeezed his hand. 'Tonight.'

'Yes,' the look in his eyes was for her alone.

'You have a lot of explaining to do,' she heard Trevor say aggressively as she let herself into the house.

She smiled to herself as she heard Dominic's soothing voice, watching them out of the kitchen window as they talked together for several minutes. Trevor didn't look any less ruffled when they finally parted, but at least they hadn't come to blows.

'I thought you'd be in bed by now,' Trevor said gruffly, locking the door behind him.

'I wanted to make sure everything was all right.'

'Well, I would hardly be likely to take a swing at Dom—he always could beat me, both verbally and physically. But I did ask you not to be long. So far tonight I've been down here for three glasses of water. I'll be floating soon.'

Alexandra giggled. 'Oh, Trevor!'

'I still don't know what's going on between you two, but Dom assures me I have nothing to worry about. Nothing to worry about!' he scorned. 'My sister-in-law disappears in the middle of the night to see my brother, she comes back here hours later looking thoroughly kissed and I'm told not to worry!' He shook his head.

'It *was* only kisses,' she told him with a blush, knowing how nearly it had been more than that.

'That's what Dom said. Oh, let's get to bed. Gail already thinks there's something wrong with me because I'm drinking so much water, and I have to get up for work in a couple of hours. By the way, Dom asked me if it was okay for him to take you out to dinner this evening. I said yes. I take it you wanted to go?'

Her eyes glowed. 'Oh yes!'

'My elder brother asking *my* permission to take you out,' he muttered. 'It's ridiculous.'

'Would you rather he hadn't asked?'

'I'm too tired to even think about it. Try not to disturb Gail on your way to bed, she doesn't even realise you've been out.' Trevor sighed. 'I hope we have a son —a daughter is too much of a worry.'

'A boy could turn out like his uncle,' she teased.

'God, yes!' He ran his hand through his hair. 'I can't win either way.'

'You'll survive,' she smiled.

He grimaced. 'I'm not so sure. I'll leave it up to you what you choose to tell Gail. I'm completely confused about the whole thing.'

Alexandra didn't know what to tell Gail either, and she pondered on it all the next day. She had told her sister that she had a dinner date that evening, but she knew Gail assumed it was John. Gail adored Dominic, but Alexandra knew she was also well aware of his reputation with women, and she wasn't sure of her reaction to her going out with him.

It was very cowardly of her, but she left it until she had prepared Gail and Trevor's evening meal, had her bath, and got herself ready to go out before saying anything to her sister. At least this way she wouldn't have to listen to the dire warnings for too long.

Tonight she was dressed as she had wanted to be last night, the black gown a gift she had treated herself to that afternoon. Dominic hadn't said it was to be formal wear, but after all, tonight was by way of being a celebration for them. And in six months there would be even more to celebrate if she had her way.

The black gown was quite simply cut, moulding to her breasts and flaring out from the waist in clinging folds that ended just below the knee. The thin ribbon shoulder-straps showed her creamy shoulders and the dark hollow between her breasts to advantage. It was a typical example of 'the little black dress' and it made her feel sophisticated—even if she wasn't.

Her hair was freshly washed and pulled back in a tight knot on top of her head, the severity of the style emphasising her high cheekbones, the brilliance of her blue eyes and the generous curve to her lips.

She went into Gail's room at almost eight o'clock to say goodnight, to find her sister propped up against the pillows reading a magazine. She put the magazine down at Alexandra's entrance, whistling appreciatively. 'Who's this for? Certainly not for John, you aren't that interested in him.' She patted the bed beside her for Alexandra to sit down.

'You're right, it isn't for John. It's——' Alexandra stopped as the doorbell rang, the sound of the two men's voices perfectly audible to them upstairs.

Gail smiled. 'It's all right, it isn't your escort. It's Dominic.'

'Yes,' Alexandra said gruffly.

'So, who are you going out with?'

'It's Dominic,' she said abruptly.

'I know, I just said——' Gail's look sharpened, changing to disbelief. 'Are you telling me you're going out with Dominic?'

'Yes.'

'I see. So you don't hate him any more?'

Alexandra gave a relieved laugh. At least Gail hadn't ridiculed her. 'I don't think I ever did, I just held a stupid grudge against him that should have been forgotten years ago.'

'And he's the reason you've been walking around the place like a pale ghost of yourself lately, not your break-up with Roger?'

'Yes.' Alexandra felt relieved now that the truth was at last coming out.

'Why didn't you just say so? You must have been worried to death!'

'That just about sums it up,' she admitted ruefully.

'You aren't going to get hurt in this?' Gail looked worried. 'You know Dominic isn't the faithful type. I don't want you to become just another of his discarded women.'

'Perhaps I'll be different,' Alexandra said lightly.

'I wonder how many of them thought the same thing,' Gail retorted dryly.

'Let's just hope I will be.' Alexandra stood up. 'I have to go now, Gail. Dominic isn't the most patient of men.'

Almost as if on cue Dominic and Trevor came into the bedroom. 'You look as if you're worth waiting for,' Dominic drawled, kissing her lightly on the cheek. 'And how is my favourite sister-in-law this evening?' He bent to kiss Gail too.

'Slightly confused at the moment.'

'Because I'm taking Alex to dinner?' he queried lightly. 'Don't worry about it, Gail. I'll make sure she isn't home late.'

'That isn't what I'm worried about!'

'It's only dinner, Gail, nothing more.' He looked at the wide gold watch on his wrist. 'We'll have to leave now—I have a table booked for nine and we have a way to drive. See you two later.'

Once in the car Alexandra gave him fleeting glances from under her long lashes, her senses spinning at how attractive he looked. The dark grey trousers fitted snugly to his thighs, his silk shirt was snowy white, the royal blue velvet jacket fitted tautly across his shoulders.

He turned to look at her. 'You're very quiet.'

'You—you made our going out together sound very trivial,' she said huskily.

'And that upset you?' he asked gently.

'Yes.'

He drove the car on to the side of the country road, switching off the engine before turning in his seat to look at her. 'I'm sorry, darling,' his thumb moved caressingly across her cheek. 'I just didn't want them to make a fuss out of it and embarrass you. Forgive me?' he asked coaxingly.

She turned her face into his hand. 'Oh, Dominic, I missed you today!'

His arm went about her shoulders and he pulled her against his side. 'I missed you too,' he said huskily, his lips against her throat. 'I've been picking up the telephone all day intending to call you and then changing my mind. Talking to you wasn't enough,' his lips claimed hers, his hands cradling each side of her face. '*God*, I needed that so badly!'

He did love her, he did, even if he wouldn't admit it yet! 'Dominic, I love you,' she told him shyly.

He smiled at her in the darkness, his face only inches away from her own. 'If you tell me that often enough I may even get to believe it.'

Alexandra raised her face so that her lips touched his. 'I'll tell you as often as you like,' she promised.

His hand was on her hair. 'How is this pinned up?'

'Why?'

'Because it looks wonderfully sophisticated, and I appreciate the fact that you're trying to look older for me, but I——'

'I am not!' she pouted. 'I was only——'

'But I prefer my wild darling,' he continued as if she hadn't spoken. 'I like to bury my face in your hair and feel its clean darkness about me.'

She pulled out the one clip holding her hair in place and shook it down about her shoulders. 'Better?'

Dominic nodded approvingly. 'Much better.' He straightened in his seat, moving away from her. 'We'd better get on, I'm not used to seducing women on roadsides.'

She laughed softly. 'Poor Dominic, reduced to the level of us other mortals!'

He restarted the car engine. 'You are a little tease, young lady,' he accused grimly.

She snuggled against him. 'Only with you, Dominic. Where are you taking me this evening?'

'To a new restaurant about twenty miles away from here. I've heard it's very good.'

Alexandra gave him a sharp look. 'Is there any reason why we have to go so far?'

'None at all, except as I said, someone told me it was a good restaurant.'

'Oh.'

He gave her a sharp look. 'Are you accusing me of trying to hide you away in dark corners?' he snapped angrily. 'Is that what you think, Alex?'

She looked abashed. 'Well, I—It did cross my mind,' she admitted reluctantly.

'Then I'll take you to the local pub tomorrow night,' he said abruptly. 'That should more than prove to you that I don't intend hiding anything.'

'It was only a thought, Dominic. I didn't——'

'Then put the thought right out of your mind,' he interrupted haughtily. 'I would be defeating the object of letting people get used to our names being linked if I didn't let people see us together. I just wanted to try this restaurant out, that's all.'

'I'm sorry, Dominic. I shouldn't even have thought such a thing.'

'No, you shouldn't,' he agreed distantly.

'I love you.' She looked at him pleadingly.

The harshness left his face, his taut body relaxed. 'Okay, we'll forget it this time. But don't think you can get round me all the time by telling me you love me. It won't work every time.'

But it had worked this time and the dinner they shared together was very enjoyable. Dominic was knowledgeable about many things and they talked ceaselessly throughout the meal, oblivious to their surroundings and to a certain extent to the food they ate, although Alexandra felt sure it was a delicious meal.

'The restaurant lives up to your friend's recommendation.' She sipped some of the wine left in her glass while Dominic enjoyed an after-dinner brandy.

'I'll tell him you said so,' he mocked.

'Him?'

'You thought it was a woman,' he guessed correctly. 'Your jealousy is a little transparent, darling. I don't have women in this area, I save that for London.'

'*Saved*,' she corrected pointedly. 'It will be the past tense, won't it?'

'After the fiasco with Sabrina, yes.'

'Is that the only reason?' she demanded. 'Because you're afraid you might fail again?'

His grey eyes watched her over the rim of his glass. 'After last night you can still ask that?'

She blushed. 'No, I'm just behaving stupidly again.'

Dominic sat forward to put his hand over the one she had resting on the table. 'I've been teasing you a little too. I knew you would assume a woman had recommended this place. Let's get out of here, I want to kiss you again.'

She smiled at him eagerly, wanting that too. She was prevented from standing up by a man walking past their table and she waited for him to pass.

'Well, well, well,' the man drawled in a slurred voice. 'If it isn't my ex-girl-friend and her new *boy*-friend,' he scorned sarcastically.

Alexandra looked up into eyes glazed by too much drink, Roger's deep brown eyes that had always seemed so gentle and kind to her in the past.

CHAPTER EIGHT

ALEXANDRA had paled considerably, but Dominic seemed unperturbed. 'Young,' he said coldly. 'I would ask you to join us, but we were just leaving.'

'Were you now,' Roger sneered. He looked contemptuously at the older man. 'I suppose it is time a child like Alexandra was home in bed.'

'Roger!' She looked around them self-consciously to see if anyone was witnessing this scene, but the other diners were either too polite to show they had heard the conversation or else they were all genuinely absorbed in their meal.

'But whose bed would it be, that's what I ask myself,' he continued insultingly.

Angry grey eyes glittered up at him. 'You're drunk, Young, or I'd put you on the floor for that remark.'

Roger tried to focus on him. 'Why? Because I know the truth about the two of you?'

'It's because you don't know the truth that I'm able to excuse your rudeness.' Dominic's words struck out like a whiplash. 'Now why don't you go home and sober up?'

'I'm sobering up right now,' Roger said dazedly. 'Probably for the first time in months. I was blinded for four months by Alexandra's apparent naïveté, only to be rudely awakened to her real nature when you began to taken an interest. I just hope you realise you're destined for the same fate. I was replaced by someone richer and more worldly, your time will probably come when she meets someone with wealth *and* youth.'

Alexandra felt sick and Dominic had gone very pale

beneath his tan. 'I want to leave now,' she said chokingly.

'You do realise I'm right, Tempest,' Roger was obviously well into the subject now. 'You're famous, a television personality, you seem exciting to Alexandra now, but once the novelty wears off she'll realise that you're twice her age, totally immoral, and play the sophisticated type of games she's only read about in dirty books.'

Dominic's mouth was a thin angry line. 'I doubt if Alex has ever read books so lewd that she could be shocked by them, and even if she has I haven't indulged in those sort of games. But I don't need to defend myself to you—Alex and I are perfectly capable of deciding our own future.'

Roger's scorn now returned to Alexandra. 'You're a child compared to the women he's known. How long do you think you'll be able to satisfy him in bed?' He shook his head. 'He's had more women than he can remember, and most of them a hell of a lot more accomplished at it than you are.'

'Dominic, can we *please* leave?' Her blue eyes were swimming with tears.

Dominic stood up, towering over the boy swaying unsteadily beside him. 'With pleasure,' he agreed grimly. 'I think your young friend has said quite enough for one evening.' He moved to pull her chair back for her. 'You go on ahead, I'll join you in a moment.'

'But——'

'Go on, Alex,' he insisted firmly. 'Wait for me outside.'

She did as he asked, waiting beside the car until he joined her a couple of minutes later. Roger had made a complete exhibition of himself and the things he had said had made her blush with embarrassment. She couldn't be sure of Dominic's reaction.

'I didn't expect you to walk all the way over here,' he said abruptly, unlocking the car door for her before going round to the other side to get in the driving seat.

'What did you say to Roger after I left?' She fidgeted with her evening bag.

'Not a lot,' he answered coldly, his attention seemingly centred on manoeuvring the car out of the car park. 'There didn't seem a lot left *to* say.'

'But you must have said something.'

'Yes,' he acknowledged tersely. 'I told him that if he ever said things like that when he was sober I'd kill him.'

She gasped, knowing he meant it. 'Dominic!'

'He has a lesson coming to him, and I'll give it to him if he ever tries anything like that again,' he promised fiercely.

That he was furiously angry she knew without a doubt, and it was all her fault. Dominic didn't like these sort of complications in his life, rebuffed boy-friends and the like, and she didn't think it would take him long to tire of such confrontations. Hadn't he just threatened to get violent with Roger if it happened again?

But she didn't want him to tire of her, although Roger's last barbs about Dominic not being satisfied with someone like her for long had gone home, painfully. Everything he had said was true; Dominic had known many women, he wasn't ashamed to admit it, and she felt sure they all were much more accomplished than she was.

How could they not be! She was so innocent that Roger's tentative attempts to touch her had put her into a complete panic. But Dominic's touch hadn't affected her the same way! The question was, would he have the patience to teach her all about love? She wasn't sure, and the uncertainty was what was tearing her apart.

They hadn't been aware of each other long enough, Dominic said; they needed time, time to get to know each other. But it was time that was her enemy now, each passing second adding to her uncertainty and nervousness.

'You've gone quiet again,' Dominic remarked, breaking into the oppressive silence that had sprung up between them.

'I—I don't know what to say.'

'No,' he agreed. 'He pretty much seems to have said it all.'

'You don't agree with him?' Her distress showed in her deep blue eyes.

Dominic glanced at her fleetingly. 'Should I?'

'Not as far as I'm concerned,' she said resentfully. 'Were the things he said about you true?'

'Which ones? That I've been with a lot of women, that to you I probably do seem to lead an exciting life, that I'm richer than he is? All of that is true.'

'That isn't the part I meant.'

'I didn't think it was,' he said tersely. 'What I want to know is did what he had to say make any impression on you?'

'In what way?' she evaded.

'In any way! God, Alex, stop being obstructive. That's only the start of it, you know. There'll probably be worse than that said, but let's hope most of it won't be said to your face. Are you going to be able to take it?'

'I don't know,' she admitted miserably.

'Now you know why I insisted on six months before we make any decision. I'm not sure you can take this type of pressure.'

'He was—he was so *nasty*!' The hurt showed in her voice.

Dominic gave a harsh laugh. 'Don't you think he has a right to be? You were going to marry him, Alex. You can't expect him to turn off the feelings he has for you just because you've changed your mind.'

'No, but——'

'There is no but, Alex,' he cut in coldly. 'Luckily I'm not made of the same stuff. If you let me down you won't be given a second chance.'

She gave him a reproachful look. 'I won't let you down. You don't have much faith in me, do you?'

'I don't have faith in any women. It's up to you to prove me wrong.'

'That's a big responsibillity,' she said nervously. 'I'm far from being infallible.'

His mouth turned back. 'I think you've more than proved that.'

'Why are you being cruel to me?' she demanded.

'At the moment I feel cruel, I feel bloody cruel! That young pup talking to me as if I'm some ageing roué who's seduced you into bed with him.'

She gave a wan smile. 'When in reality I'm the one who did the seducing. Roger would be very shocked if he knew how shamelessly I've thrown myself at you.' She put her hand on his thigh. 'I wish we could hide away from the world during the next six months and face everyone again when we're married.' She felt him tense beneath her touch but didn't remove her hand.

Some of the anger left his face. 'I could think of ways to occupy you for six months,' he agreed softly. 'But hiding is the one thing I don't intend doing. Could you stop doing that!' he asked tautly as she caressed his thigh with circular movements.

'Why?' She watched him beneath lowered lashes.

'Because if you don't you could become the first girl I've ever tried to rape in the confines of a car.' He took a deep ragged breath.

'It wouldn't be rape.'

'The way I feel right now it would. Stop it, Alex! Don't play games.'

'The games Roger was talking about?' she teased.

Dominic frowned. 'And that's another thing! Does he

think I go to orgies every night or something?'

Still she caressed him. 'Oh, not every night,' she shook her head. 'Just every other night,' she added mischievously.

'That sort of sex isn't my scene at all. I like to wake up in the morning able to remember who I slept with the night before.'

'You'll know in the future, it will either be me or no one.'

He gave a husky laugh. 'You're very sure of yourself.'

'I have to be—you don't have any confidence in me at all.'

'At least you're able to laugh about it now. I'm finding it a little more difficult to accept what he said about me. Alex, will you please stop that!' he groaned at her continued caressing. 'I can just imagine us parked on the side of the road with me trying to explain to a policeman how *you* seduced *me*. I somehow don't think he would believe me.'

'Poor Dominic,' she taunted, 'taken advantage of by a mere girl.'

'I could always stop the car and give you a good hiding,' he threatened.

Alexandra pouted at him mischievously. 'Don't you like me to touch you?'

'Yes,' he said through gritted teeth. 'But not while I'm trying to drive.'

'All right,' she removed her hand. 'I'll wait until we get home.'

'Not if Trevor decides to come outside and meet us again you won't, not after I've assured him that nothing like that will happen between us.'

'I meant your house.'

'We aren't going back to my house,' he told her firmly.

'But it's only eleven o'clock, much too early to take me home.'

'I promised Gail I would make sure you weren't home late.'

'But it isn't late,' she insisted petulantly. 'I want to be alone with you.'

'That's what I'm afraid of.' Dominic smiled at her hurt expression. 'You know why. I'm not safe left alone with you, or rather, you're not safe alone with me.'

'But I want to be kissed.'

'I know what you want,' Dominic said gruffly. 'But you've been kissed once tonight, that will have to do. We're there now anyway.' He halted the car in the driveway. 'Meet me for lunch tomorrow and then I'll take you shopping,' he suggested.

'Lunch at your house,' she said eagerly.

'No,' he tapped her playfully on the nose. 'Lunch in town before you drag me round the shops.'

'Don't you even trust yourself alone with me during the day?'

'I don't trust *you* at any time,' he grinned at her indignation.

'So I noticed,' she retorted dryly. 'You haven't even switched off the car engine.'

'That's because I don't intend stopping,' he teased her.

'Aren't you coming in for coffee?' She gave him a sly look. 'My dates usually come in for coffee.'

'Do they indeed,' he drawled. 'Then I suppose I'd better follow suit.' He switched off the engine. 'We have to do this properly. It's years since I had a girl-friend as such, I'll need a little coaching as to the right procedure.'

'I've offered to do that, but you keep refusing me.'

'Out, young lady! I'll have one cup of coffee and then I'm leaving, ten minutes at most.'

Alexandra let them into the house with her own key,

Trevor having left the kitchen light on for her. 'How do you like your coffee?' she asked in a whisper.

'Black, no sugar,' Dominic whispered back.

'You go into the lounge and I'll bring it through in a moment,' she told him softly.

She joined him in the lounge a few minutes later, putting down the tray before going over to close the door. 'Here,' she handed him a cup of steaming coffee.

Dominic sat forward on the sofa. 'Why are we whispering?'

Alexandra grinned at him. 'That's half the fun.'

He raised his eyebrows. 'I don't find it fun, I'll probably get a sore throat.'

She curled up on the sofa next to him, her head on his shoulder. 'There's no romance in your soul. It makes it more illicit this way.'

He turned to kiss her. 'It already feels illicit enough, thank you.'

Her mouth lingered on his. 'Mm, that was nice.'

'Nice!' he scorned. 'I don't want you to think my kisses *nice.*'

She turned into his arms, her mouth raised invitingly. 'Then show me what they can be like,' she said throatily. 'Go on, put your coffee down and prove to me that you're the man you once said I'd meet.'

He laughed, putting her away from him. 'That won't work, Alex. I've been tempted by experts. You'll have to do more than that.'

'I would if you would let me.'

'Well, I won't.' He stood up, the coffee forgotten. 'Goodnight, Alex. Twelve o'clock tomorrow. Be ready.'

'*Dominic,*' she peered at him over the back of the sofa. 'You aren't leaving me?'

The light was suddenly switched off, leaving the room bathed in moonlight. 'No,' he agreed with a groan. 'No, I'm not leaving you, not yet.' He came back to her side.

'You're wild and untamed and no one should ever be allowed to clip your wings. Marriage to Roger Young would have stifled you.' He smoothed her hair back from her face. 'I won't stifle you, darling.'

'I know you won't.'

'We're whispering again.'

'I know,' her eyes glowed. 'But it's a different type of whispering.'

His lips moved across her cheek to linger on her parted lips. 'I want you! I've been wanting you all evening and you haven't been making it easy for me to fight you.'

Alexandra lay back on the sofa, pulling him with her. She touched the hair on the nape of his neck. 'Did I tell you how handsome you look?'

'No.'

'Well, you do. But you always do, always. Oh, Dominic,' her breath caught in her throat, 'why didn't I realise sooner that I love you?'

'Because you didn't love me sooner.'

'But I did. I did!'

'No,' he denied gently. 'I can tell you the exact moment you became aware of me. It was the day after Young had made that pass at you in your bedroom. You came back from visiting Gail and I was in the lounge.'

'Yes, yes, I remember.' Alexandra remembered the way her body had reacted to him and the way she had been angry with herself. She blushed. 'It was the way you looked at me.'

'Mentally undressing you,' he said with remembered humour.

'Well, you were.'

'I know,' he acknowledged unashamedly. 'I'd always thought of you as Gail's kid sister, a pain in the neck most of the time, and to see someone kissing you with passion put you in an entirely different light as far as I was concerned.' His hold about her tightened. 'I didn't like seeing him touch you.'

'He never touched me like you do.'

'No,' he agreed tautly. 'You allow me far too many liberties than are good for me. Like now,' he slipped one of the thin straps off her shoulder, caressing her skin with his tongue. 'I like your body—what I've seen of it.'

'Dominic!' she burrowed into his shoulder.

'Yes—Dominic!' He kissed her briefly on the lips before getting to his feet. 'I suppose I have to sneak out of the house now?' he mocked.

'You aren't leaving?' she asked in dismay.

'I am.' He straightened his jacket.

'But——'

He silenced her with a look. 'No, Alex.'

'You're no fun,' she said sulkily.

His grey eyes hardened to angry pebbles. 'I could give you so much fun it would frighten the hell out of you!' he rasped. 'Now, I'm going because I don't want to do exactly that.'

'Frighten me?'

'That, amongst other things. Don't bother to see me out, I know the way.'

Alexandra had to run to keep up with his angry pace. 'Are we still going out tomorrow?'

'Is there any reason why we shouldn't be?' he returned coldly.

'I—I wasn't sure.'

'I said twelve o'clock and I meant twelve o'clock.'

She was left standing in the doorway as he drove off without another word, leaving her knowing what an unpredictable man she had fallen in love with. One minute he was the ardent lover, the next a cold stranger.

She switched off the lights and slowly made her way up to her bedroom. All in all it had been a pretty dis-

astrous evening. Up until Roger's interruption she had
thought things were going reasonably well, but after that
he seemed to have put a blight on the evening. And now
Dominic had left her in a bad mood.

'Is that you, Alexandra?' Gail called from her bedroom.

'Yes,' she replied dully.

'Did you have a nice evening?'

'Yes, thank you.'

'Could the two of you talk about this in the morning?'
came Trevor's sleepy interruption. 'Some of us are trying to sleep.'

'But I wanted——'

'In the morning, Gail,' he said sternly.

But when morning came there was little Alexandra
could tell Gail about the previous evening, especially
as she wasn't really sure Dominic would arrive to take
her out for lunch. A couple of times she was tempted
to telephone him and find out, but each time she changed
her mind. She had done enough running after him the
last few days, she couldn't keep doing it.

But she needn't have worried, for he turned up
promptly at twelve o'clock, laughing and joking with
Gail and Trevor. There was a certain reserve about him
when he spoke to her, but the other two didn't seem to
be aware of it.

Alexandra's hair swung down to her shoulders in
deep natural waves, her blue eyes sparklingly clear in
the midday sunshine. The thin blue knitted dress was a
perfect foil for her black hair and was the exact colour
of her eyes, but for all the notice Dominic took of her
appearance she might not have bothered.

'It's a lovely day, isn't it?' she broached once they
were out in the car.

'Yes.' He appeared to be intent on driving the car.

'Where are we going for lunch?'

'I thought maybe a pub,' he said disinterestedly.

'Oh, lovely!' she gave him a glowing smile.

'You're easily pleased,' he said tersely.

'Yes, I am, aren't I!' Tears glittered in her eyes at his continued coldness. 'I must be if I can still sit here with you when you treat me so distantly. You're a cold, heartless bully, Dominic. I haven't done anything, except ask for your love, and I don't see what's so wrong about that.'

'Don't you?' he asked grimly.

'No, I don't!' She turned angrily in her seat. 'What's the matter with you? You're completely unfathomable!'

He gave a deep sigh. 'Maybe I've decided I don't like the responsibility of having someone else's feelings mixed up in my life after all.'

Her mouth was suddenly dry. 'And have you?'

He shrugged. 'Maybe.'

'Then stop the car right now and I'll get out. You're a coward, Dominic. The life you lead, the job you do, anyone would expect you to be brave and fearless, but when it comes to personal relationships you really lose out. This might seem a ridiculous thing to say, but you're afraid of life!'

His mouth was a thin angry line. 'You don't know what you're talking about.'

'Yes, I do! You were hurt once, so you don't want to get involved again. If that isn't running away from life I don't know what is,' she scorned.

'I wasn't *hurt* by Marianne,' he said with disdain. 'I loathed and detested her.'

'But you——'

'I was never in love with her. She told me she was having my baby, and I was stupid enough to take her word for it. When I realised she'd taken me for a fool I was disgusted and sickened. I didn't touch her again. That's why I was more out of the country than in it, I had nothing to keep me here. Ten months after we were married Marianne told me she was pregnant.' His mouth turned back in a sneer. 'She expected me to father it.'

'But you were her husband.'

'Like hell I was! I couldn't bear to touch her, I hadn't been near her for five or six months. I knew I couldn't be the father, and although I'd continued the charade of the marriage I wasn't going to be a party to that. We were divorced and she eventually married the father of the child.'

'I didn't know,' said Alexandra in a hushed voice. 'I naturally assumed——'

'Like most other people you assumed that I was to blame for our divorce,' he finished bitterly. 'But you're right about one thing. I am afraid, I'm afraid of domesticity and all it entails.'

'I've already told you that you don't have to marry me,' she reminded him.

'And you think Trevor would settle for that, for you moving in with me?'

'I wouldn't ask him.'

'You're a damned little fool!' Dominic turned off down one of the side roads, parking the car amongst the trees and out of view of other travellers. 'You damned little fool,' he repeated agonisingly. 'I don't deserve you, Alex. You're too innocent and vulnerable for me to trample on.'

'Then don't trample on me.'

He ran a hand through his blond hair. 'I can't seem to help it.'

'Would you prefer to take me home?'

'No!' he denied sharply, grasping her arms painfully. 'I lay awake all night wondering why I walked out on you last night. I think it was what you said about my not being fun. That was Marianne's constant cry because I refused to sleep with her.'

'Oh God, and I did the same thing.' Alexandra's face was very pale. 'I'm sorry, Dominic.'

'No, *I'm* sorry.' He pulled her savagely into his arms. 'I've been in hell all night, thinking I might have lost you. I have a hell of a temper and I took it out on you because you said something that reminded me of the past. You're nothing like Marianne, and yet when you said that to me I just saw red.'

'I didn't know, I didn't realise. I was only teasing you.'

'I know,' Dominic groaned into her hair. 'But I paid for my temper with a sleepless night. I'm sorry if I hurt you, darling.'

'I was more confused than hurt,' she confessed. 'I couldn't think what I'd done.'

'You hadn't done a thing.' He cradled each side of her face. 'Do you think you'll be able to stand my foul moods?'

Alexandra smiled at him uncertainly. 'As long as you make love to me afterwards.'

'As I would like to do right now,' he groaned as if in pain. 'That isn't helping my temper, I'm afraid, the fact that I'm trying to control my desire for you.'

She leant forward to kiss him on the lips. 'Then I'll help you.'

'Not like that you won't!'

'Exactly like this,' she murmured against his mouth.

'You're pushing me over the edge again.' He watched her as if mesmerised as she slowly unbuttoned his shirt to reveal his hair-roughened chest, running her fingertips lightly over his heated skin. 'Alex!' his mouth moved over her throat.

'I'm not going to stop, Dominic. You're the one denying yourself, not me. I've always dreamt of having a husband, a home of my own, children,' her voice softened. 'But they aren't that important to me that I would risk losing you to have them. I could have had all that with Roger, but I would rather have a few months with you than nothing at all.'

'Oh, darling,' he moaned. 'Don't make it so easy for me, make me sweat a little. I should be grovelling to you for the moods I take you through, for the way I turn on you at the slightest provocation. If it wasn't for the fact that you have a temper yourself I would walk all over you.'

Her hands were inside his shirt. 'We make quite a fiery combination,' she whispered.

'You'll still marry me?'

She shook her head. 'Marriage isn't what you want.' She kissed his chest. 'This is what you want,' her mouth travelled up his throat, lingering on his strong jawline before hesitating near his mouth. 'Isn't it, Dominic?'

'*Yes!* Yes, yes, *yes!*' He pushed her back against the leather upholstery, crushing her beneath him. But she felt no pain, only a fierce gladness to be in his arms.

'Then take it, Dominic darling,' she encouraged. 'Take it!'

'I think I may have to,' he groaned.

Alexandra offered no resistance as he forced her mouth apart, his hands ran freely over her body, the sudden rush of feeling in his body for her an indication of his desire.

He pushed aside the rounded neckline of her woollen dress, his mouth trembling with passion against her creamy breasts. Their bodies fused together, desperately clamouring for full consummation, the barrier of their clothing the only thing stopping them.

Dominic touched her thigh beneath her dress, caressing the smoothness of her skin, setting her afire where he touched. She gasped as his mouth claimed her breast, his lips bringing it to full pulsating life, the whole of her body feeling posessed by him, engulfed by him.

'Dominic!' She felt as if a tide was rising up inside

her, flashing pleasure and pain, and a feeling that a dam was about to burst and consume them both, shooting her body into racking pleasure.

She arched against him, all her senses crying out for the deep overwhelming pleasure that must surely be hers if he continued his caresses. He mustn't stop now, not now she was so close—so close to what? She had no idea, but she knew once it had happened she would truly know the reason she had been born, would know the pleasure of being made into a woman by the man she loved.

'Oh, Dominic, I love you!' she gasped her feelings. 'I love you!'

He seemed not to have heard her, his blond head bent with serious intentness over the beauty of her body, her breasts bare to his hungry gaze. His grey eyes were almost black, their depths glassy, a strange vulnerability to his passion-giving mouth.

Suddenly he clutched her to him, a choked sound in his throat as he shuddered in her arms. 'I can't make love to you here!' he moaned, his forehead on hers. 'I can't do that to you! When I make you mine I want it to be done with no uncertainty between us. I want to take you as my wife, not like this.'

Alexandra could feel the desire slowly leaving his body. 'But we just agreed that marriage isn't what you want.'

'With you it is.' He searched her flushed face, gently touching her bruised lips. 'I hurt you,' he kissed her tenderly. 'I'm sorry.'

'Don't be. I——' she blushed, 'I liked it.'

Dominic sat up, pulling her with him. 'I know,' he gave a rueful smile. 'I guess it's another cold shower for me. I seem to have done nothing else the last three days, and all they've done is give me a cold.' His look deepened. 'They certainly don't have the desired effect.

As soon as I see you again my temperature shoots through the ceiling.'

Alexandra straightened her dress in her embarrassment. 'I don't think this dress will ever be the same.' She tried without success to get some shape back into the neckline.

Dominic chuckled. 'I'll buy you a new one.'

'You most certainly will not!'

He raised one eyebrow. 'Why not?'

'Because I don't want gifts from you. Why are we going to the shops this afternoon anyway? Do you have something you want to buy?'

He shrugged, completely composed now, a certain rakishness in his appearance the only sign he showed of the passionate embrace they had just shared. 'Only if I see something. I'm just trying to act like any other boyfriend. I'm sure Young took you shopping on Saturdays.'

'Well, yes, but——'

'Then so will I. But lunch first.' He gave her a teasing look. 'I seem to have worked up an appetite.' He laughed as she blushed anew.

They had lunch in a pub as Dominic had suggested, Dominic enjoying steak while Alexandra had a prawn salad. After their meal they sat outside in the garden, enjoying a cool drink before going on their way.

It was while waiting outside a shop for Dominic that she saw Roger's mother. Her face lit up in greeting, but she received only a cold stare in return.

Alexandra frowned. 'Good afternoon, Mrs Young.'

'Alexandra,' she nodded distantly.

'You're well, I hope?' Alexandra persisted.

'Thank you, yes.'

'And Mr Young, is he——' she broke off as she saw Mrs Young's attention wander to something over her shoulder, her face at once stiff and unyielding. Alexandra turned to see Dominic making his way down the street towards her, his handsomeness and natural arrogance attracting attention to him from passers by.

'So you're here with him!' Mrs Young hissed. 'My boy isn't good enough for you now, is he, not now you have *him* interested. It's disgusting, absolutely disgusting!' With a last disdainful look in Alexandra's direction she walked off.

Dominic put his arm about her shoulders and dropped a small parcel into her hand. 'For you.'

She was still deathly pale from her encounter with Mrs Young. 'What is it?'

'Open it and see.'

She pulled off the wrapping paper to reveal a jewellery case, snapping open the lid to reveal a bracelet of delicate gold, five diamonds sparkling on its surface. 'It's lovely, Dominic,' she took it out of its box. 'Really beautiful! But you shouldn't have bought it for me.'

'Consider it an early birthday present.' He noticed her pale face for the first time. 'Hey, what's wrong?'

She gave a wan smile. 'I just met Mrs Young.'

He nodded his head in understanding. 'And she made her feelings clear concerning the severing of your friendship with her son,' he guessed correctly.

'Yes,' Alexandra said huskily.

'Come on, let's get you home. I think you've had enough for one day'

They didn't mention Mrs Young again, talking of other subjects on their way home. But Alexandra couldn't dismiss it as easily as Dominic appeared to have done. She knew now what he had meant about people's nastiness. But at least each encounter was hurting less and less, until she felt sure she would become immune to these attacks altogether.

She was laughing with Dominic as they entered the house, the laughter soon turning to stunned silence as an ear-splitting scream filled the air.

'What the hell——' Dominic moved forward.

Trevor appeared at the top of the stairs, a pale-faced, wild-haired Trevor with tears in his eyes. 'It's Gail,' he choked. 'Something has gone wrong—the baby's coming now. Oh God, something's gone wrong!' he cried as another scream rang out.

CHAPTER NINE

'My God!' Dominic was almost as white as Trevor.
'Have you called for an ambulance?'

'Of course I have. But I don't know if she can be
moved.'

'Can't you do something?' Alexandra demanded,
pushing past the two of them. 'Listen to the pain she's
in!'

'I have been, for the last fifteen minutes,' Trevor said
in a strangulated voice.

She clutched at his arm. 'I'm sorry, so sorry. I'll go
in to her.'

'Trevor?' Dominic prompted his brother.

'Yes, yes, go in,' he said as if in a dream. 'I'll just go
down and call the ambulance again. I told them it was
an emergency, they should have been here by now.' He
ran down the stairs.

'Go with him, Dominic,' Alexandra encouraged. 'He
looks at breaking point.'

'I'm not surprised. Hell, I couldn't go through this.'
There was torture in Dominic's eyes. 'If we ever get
married we aren't having children.'

If, if, *if*! There were too many ifs and buts about
their relationship. 'Now isn't the time to discuss it,
Dominic. Just go down with Trevor. He may be a
doctor, but it's a little different when it's your own
wife.'

'She's your sister.'

'I'll manage.'

Alexandra wasn't quite so confident when she actually
got into the bedroom with Gail. The pain her sister

was in was excruciating, it was there in her fever-bright eyes and the way her knees were drawn up into her body.

'Oh, my God!' she gasped as another pain racked her body, and gripped Alexandra's hand as if it were a lifeline. She relaxed her hold as the pain subsided. 'Sorry,' she looked down at the hand she had squeeed the blood out of. 'I'm being such a nuisance.'

Alexandra stood up, going into the adjoining bathroom to wet the flannel and place it on Gail's heated forehead. 'The baby is just in a hurry to be born, that's all.'

'I don't know if he's going to be born at all,' Gail said brokenly.

'Of course he is,' Alexandra said briskly.

Gail smiled wanly. 'I'm not silly, Alexandra dear. I haven't been a doctor's wife for the last three years without learning something. Besides, Trevor never panics. He's always so calm and reliable, something he isn't at the moment.'

'He's never been a father before,' Alexandra excused.

'No,' her sister agreed slowly. 'But something is wrong, I'm sure of it. The pains shouldn't have come on so quickly or so fiercely.'

Trevor appeared in the open doorway. 'The ambulance is on its way—apparently the first one got stopped at a road accident.' He came to his wife's side, holding her hand. 'It will be all right now, darling, we'll soon have you in hospital. Go down and keep Dominic company, Alexandra. I'll stay with Gail now.'

She knew he wanted to be alone with his wife, so she did as he suggested, and found Dominic in the lounge, a large glass of whisky in his hand.

His face was haggard. 'Would you like one?' he indicated the liquid.

Considering the size of the glass and the amount in it

she thought he would be well over the limit by the time he had drunk it, and it might not even be his first one. She shook her head. 'I think one of us ought to be capable of driving.'

'Mm?'

'Well, we can't all go to the hospital in the ambulance —Trevor probably, but we'll have to drive there.'

Dominic put a hand up to his neck as if it ached. 'I didn't think of that,' he rasped.

'Does Trevor know what's wrong?'

'He says the baby is the wrong way round, breech birth or something like that.' He gulped down some of the whisky.

'Oh no!' her dismay was obvious.

'What does it mean?' he asked.

'I don't really know that much about it, but I think it means that the baby isn't going to be born head first. They may even have to operate.'

'No wonder he's going through hell,' muttered Dominic.

'I think that's the ambulance now.' Alexandra hurried to the door. 'But Trevor isn't even sure if it's safe to move her.'

'Well, they can't operate here!'

'They may have to.' She hurried out to let in the ambulance men and the doctor who had accompanied them, showing them straight up to the bedroom.

She and Dominic waited anxiously downstairs while the two doctors consulted. Trevor was a trained doctor, but the man with him was a specialist in maternity cases. Alexandra just hoped that they would decide Gail could be taken to the hospital where they had all the facilities to help her.

'What on earth are they doing up there!' Dominic snapped, as the murmur of voices seemed to go on for ever. 'Why don't they do something and stop talking about it?'

'Calm down, Dominic,' Alexandra soothed him. 'Anyone would think it was your wife having the baby!' she
attempted to tease him, her own tension very high.

'I'm never going to put any woman through that.'

It was the second time he had said something like
this. 'It isn't usually like that,' she told him gently.

As they heard Gail cry out again he gave a shudder.
'Never!' he said harshly.

Trevor came into the room. 'We're going to get her to
the hospital now. They're going to try and turn the baby
round when we get there. It's too late to stop the labour,
the baby is going to be born today, one way or the
other.'

It took quite a lot to get Dominic to let Alexandra
drive his Ferrari, but he finally gave in, giving her in-
structions all the way to the hospital. She didn't argue
with him, realising he needed this outlet to the despair
he felt, knowing the deep affection he had for Gail.

The hospital waiting-room was white and stark and
they were both too worried to bother with the magazines
scattered over the table. Gail had been taken into the
delivery room and Trevor had gone in with her, leaving
them to sit here and wait.

'It always seems so quiet in these places,' Dominic
remarked moodily, gazing sightlessly out of the window.

'You aren't very good in a crisis,' Alexandra told him
truthfully.

'Not when it's someone I care about. Gail is like a
sister to me.'

'Well, she *is* my sister,' she choked.

Instantly he was by her side, cradling her to him. 'I'm
sorry, Alex, I'm a thoughtless swine. It's just that it all
happened so quickly. One minute we were out shopping,
the next—well, here we are.'

She looked at the bracelet on her wrist. 'I don't think

I thanked you for this.'

'You were upset,' he said understandingly .

'Yes. It's a little premature as a birthday present,' she remarked, remembering his excuse for giving it to her.

'It's a bauble, nothing more.'

'An expensive bauble.'

'I like expensive things—especially on beautiful women.'

'Flatterer!'

'I have to have something to recommend me,' he said dryly.

'You have a lot more than that,' she told him throatily. 'And I like my gift, even if I did ask you not to buy me anything.'

'I'll buy what I damn well please! You're——' he broke off as Trevor staggered into the room. 'My God, what's happened now?'

Trevor dropped down into a chair. 'The baby won't be turned round.' He looked at them with tortured blue eyes. 'They may have to either save Gail or the baby.'

'Oh no!' Alexandra felt sick.

'You told them to save Gail,' Dominic muttered.

'Well, of course I did,' Trevor said impatiently, as if there had been no need for that question. 'But Gail is insisting they save the baby. She keeps crying for them to save the baby,' his voice broke. 'It's breaking me up!'

'Hell, man, she can't mean it,' Dominic burst out savagely. 'She can have other babies, but there's only one Gail.'

'I know, I know.' Trevor stood up. 'I have to get back now, I'll let you know about—about—I'll let you know,' and he hurried from the room.

'God, I feel so useless!' Dominic cried angrily. 'There's absolutely nothing I can do. I don't like being in this type of situation.'

'Stop it, Dominic!' said Alexandra sharply. 'Other

people have to go through this, just think how Trevor must be feeling. He's a doctor and yet there's nothing he can do either. He just has to sit and wait like the rest of us.'

'Oh, Alex!' He pulled her into the circle of his arms. 'Why do women choose to go through this?'

'We don't all choose to, although Gail did. Please don't worry, Dominic,' she smoothed back his tousled hair.

'You would never put me through this?'

'I can't promise that, it wouldn't be fair to ask me.'

'But children aren't a necessity in marriage,' he said stubbornly. 'At least, not in mine.'

'We aren't married yet,' she reminded him.

'True.'

'You're letting this colour your judgment. And this isn't exactly the right time to be discussing this, not when Gail is in there fighting for her life. I—I just want to sit quietly.'

'Like you said, I'm not acting very well in this.' His look was distant. 'I'll be back later.'

Alexandra looked at him dazedly. 'Where are you going?'

'Outside, anywhere away from here.'

'But you can't. You can't!'

'I'll be back soon, Alexandra. I just have to get some air.'

She couldn't believe he had really gone. He was acting out of character, not the usual strong dependable Dominic she had come to expect. This was a very serious time for all of them, but it shouldn't have affected Dominic this badly.

He hadn't returned by the time a tired but triumphant Trevor came into the waiting-room. 'It's a boy, Alexandra! A beautiful healthy living baby boy,' he shouted, his face wreathed in smiles. 'And Gail is going to be fine too.'

'Did they have to operate?' she asked.

'It was the only way. But they're both alive, Alexandra! Isn't it wonderful?'

'Really wonderful,' she agreed tearfully. 'Can I see her?'

He shook his head. 'Not just now, she's sleeping. She won't be sensible again until morning. Where's Dominic?'

'He couldn't stand the tension a moment longer, he's gone for a walk,' she excused.

'I don't blame him. But Gail was so brave, so brave. And the baby is beautiful,' Trevor glowed.

'He won't thank you for that when he's older,' she teased.

'You have to see him, Alexandra. He's been taken down to the nursery.'

'Dominic will wonder where we've gone,' she pointed out reasonably.

'No, I won't,' he said from behind them. 'I gather everything is okay?' he spoke to his brother.

'Just great,' Trevor beamed. 'Come down to the nursery and see my son. Gail can't be disturbed at the moment—She needs all the rest she can get.'

Alexandra and Dominic duly admired the new member of their family, although at the moment he looked like all the other babies in their cots, certainly not the cause of all the trauma his birth had caused as he slept peacefully through other babies crying.

Dominic stood watching him from his great height. 'I don't suppose he has a name yet?'

'Oh yes, he does,' laughed Trevor, obviously very relieved that the danger was over. 'Gail managed to be very firm about that before they put her completely under. His name is Alexander Dominic,' he informed them proudly.

'I'm flattered,' his brother smiled.

Alexandra was more than flattered. It sounded

strangely right to hear the male version of her name and Dominic's linked together in this way, curiously intimate.

'It's a lovely name,' she told Trevor breathlessly.

'We thought so.' By this time they were back at the waiting-room. 'I'll have to go and sort out some accommodation again,' he said ruefully. 'I don't think I'll be very popular, moving in and out of here as if it's a hotel.'

'You're moving back to the hospital?' It was something that hadn't occurred to her.

'I shall have to, Gail will be in here for a few weeks. I want to be close to her and the baby.'

'Does that mean Alexandra has to move back in with me?' Dominic enquired distantly.

She looked at him sharply, realising for the first time that he hadn't spoken to her directly since he had come back from his walk in the hospital grounds. He suddenly seemed to have shut her out again, become the arrogant stranger of the past.

'If you wouldn't mind,' Trevor answered vaguely. 'She can't be left alone in the house.'

'I wouldn't mind ...' Alexandra began.

'I believe we've had this argument once before, Alexandra,' Dominic said coldly. 'And the outcome will be the same.'

Alexandra! He had called her Alexandra for the second time within the space of a few minutes. Something was wrong, very wrong. She felt the fear rising up within her.

'I can stay at the house,' she said softly once she and Dominic were on their way, leaving a jubilant Trevor arranging for his room at the hospital.

'The matter is settled.' His voice was clipped and abrupt.

'But I—— It's different this time. We—You—I—'

'Yes?' he snapped.

'Nothing,' she mumbled.

'You were going to say something, Alexandra.'

There it was again! 'It isn't important.'

'Very well,' he seemed to consider the matter closed. 'Do you want me to take you home to collect your clothing?'

'Yes, please.' She looked down at her hands, aware that things had changed dramatically between them. 'I'll drive over later in my own car.'

'I'll drive you back now.'

'No!' she answered more sharply than she intended. 'No, I'll bring my car over. I'll need transport.'

'Okay,' he nodded. 'I'll see you later, then.'

She looked at him pleadingly. 'Why don't you come in and talk to me while I pack?'

'I have some work to do. I've been neglecting it lately.'

'Oh.' Alexandra knew who was to blame for that. She got out of the car. 'I won't be long.'

Dominic nodded coolly. 'I'll tell Charles to prepare a room for you.'

Somewhere between going to the hospital and leaving again she had lost him, she knew it as surely as she knew her own name. She didn't know how it had happened, why it had happened, but the Dominic who had returned from his walk had not been the same Dominic who had kissed her with such passion this morning.

And she couldn't begin to understand what had made him change. He had always been an elusive man, but she had really thought he was seriously interested in her, his whole attitude had indicated as much. But he had never once said he loved her, had never once made that final commitment!

Now she didn't think he ever would. He had gone away from her, either temporarily or permanently, and she didn't know how she was going to bear his coldness towards her after the passion they had shared.

She arrived at Dominic's house just before dinner, admitted by the inscrutable Charles. He unbent enough to say how pleased he was for Trevor and Gail on the birth of their son before showing her to the room she had occupied on her last visit here.

'Mr Tempest will not be dining in the dining-room,' Charles told her haughtily. 'But dinner will be served to you in there when you are ready.'

'Has Dom—— Mr Tempest gone out?'

'No, Miss Paige. Mr Tempest is in the study working. He requires only a tray.'

'I see.' Alexandra tried not to show how hurt she was. 'Do you know if he'll be working long?' Her voice was a whisper.

'I have no idea. Would you like me to enquire?'

'No! Oh no, that won't be necessary.' She gave him a bright smile. 'I wouldn't want you to disturb him on my account.'

'What time will you require dinner?'

'I—I don't think I'll bother.' She unlocked her suit-case and pretended an interest in its contents. 'I'm not really hungry.'

'I'm sure Mr Tempest wouldn't approve of you not having dinner,' Charles said with a frown.

She didn't give a damn whether Mr Tempest approved or not! 'Mr Tempest doesn't have to be told. After all, he's busy working.'

'Are you sure we can't tempt you with something? Some soup, a little chicken salad perhaps?'

'No, thank you, Charles,' she said firmly.

'Very well, Miss Paige. But if you change your mind you have only to ring.'

'Thank you.'

So Dominic was back to ignoring her existence, was he? She wanted to march down the stairs and demand his attention, but she daren't. If she did that he might verbally tell her that everything was over between them, and until that actually happened she had something to cling on to.

She didn't see him all that evening or the next morning for that matter. Charles informed her that 'Mr Tempest' was still working in his study, although he had taken time out to visit Gail, her sister had told her when she herself went to the hospital.

The baby was lying quietly in his cot next to Gail's bed, his little hands curled about his blanket, his blond hair fluffy and fine.

Alexandra couldn't stop looking at him. 'He's lovely,' she smiled tenderly.

'Isn't he just?' Gail sat propped up against the pillows. 'Although I didn't think so an hour or so ago. He simply wouldn't stop crying when Dominic was here, and I so wanted Dominic to like him.'

'I'm sure he liked him anyway.' Alexandra touched the soft little hand. So Dominic had once again visited Gail without telling her. This more than anything else showed her they had lost all intimacy between them. 'The poor little mite was probably hungry.'

Gail blushed. 'I knew that, but I couldn't very well feed him in front of Dominic. It would probably have embarrassed him.'

'But why? Oh—Oh, I see,' Alexandra laughed. 'Yes, I think it would have embarrassed him.'

Her sister laughed too. 'I think he got the message in the end. He left in a hurry, anyway.'

That could have been because he had suspected *she* would turn up some time this afternoon, but she didn't say that to Gail. 'We were all very worried about you yesterday,' she told her sister. 'You gave us quite a fright.'

'So Trevor told me. But the baby was worth it.'

'I'm very flattered by your choice of name, by the way.'

'Er—— Did you know Dominic was going to town tomorrow?'

Alexandra kept all emotion out of her face, although the information had given her a nasty jolt. 'No,' she said brightly. 'He'll probably tell me later.'

'He's not just going for the day, Alexandra. He says he has to go back to record some last-minute programmes.'

'And you don't believe him?' How long was he going away for? Oh, he was so cruel!

Gail looked at her closely. 'Do you?'

Alexandra's blue eyes were purple in depth, her pain evident. 'No,' she admitted brokenly. 'Oh, maybe it's true that he has the programmes to do, things must have become a bit backlogged during his absence, but I don't believe he really needs to absent himself like this.'

'Have things gone wrong between the two of you so early?' Gail couldn't hide her concern.

She gave a fleeting smile. 'I don't know. He suddenly seemed to change.'

Gail nodded. 'He's like that, he leads a very independent existence.'

'I'm just beginning to realise that.' Alexandra gave her young nephew one last lingering look, wondering if she herself would ever have children. If she couldn't have Dominic's children then she didn't want any at all. 'I'd better be going, you both need your rest.'

'You're all right, aren't you, Alexandra?' Her sister gave her an intent look. 'Dominic hasn't hurt you too badly?'

'He hasn't hurt me at all,' she replied briskly. 'We only went out a couple of times.'

'Yes, but——'

'Don't fuss, Gail! I'm grown up, you have another

baby to take care of now.'

'Yes, and he's a darling.'

Alexandra laughed. 'I hope you still feel that way when he wakes you up screaming for his food in the middle of the night! They're being kind to you at the moment, letting you sleep right through, but once you get over the operation they'll start wheeling him in here all hours of the night.'

'Horror!'

'Just warning you of things to come.'

'And enjoying doing it,' teased Gail.

'Of course,' Alexandra chuckled. 'See you tomorrow.'

Dominic was in the lounge when she returned, although he looked no less forbidding than he had yesterday. She wasn't even sure she should go into the room, he didn't look as if he would welcome her interruption to his solitude.

She sat down wordlessly, watching his averted face, the smoke from his cheroot like a shroud about him. Finally she couldn't stand the silence any longer. 'Gail told me you're going up to London tomorrow.'

'Yes.'

'How long for?'

'I have no idea,' he said coldly, still not looking at her.

'You must have some idea, Dominic. You—— I'm sorry,' she bowed her head, 'I shouldn't have said that.'

He shrugged his broad shoulders. 'No, you shouldn't,' he agreed.

'But you——'

For the first time he looked at her, his grey eyes steely, nothing of the lover about him. 'If you have something to say, Alexandra, then say it. It's a little tiresome having you starting to say things and never finishing them.'

How could she say anything to him when he called

her Alexandra so coldly? 'I'm sorry,' she muttered miserably.

He stood up with force, the fitted navy blue trousers and shirt emphasising his tan and the blondness of his hair. 'And I'm a little tired of you saying sorry every two minutes too,' he snapped, his eyes narrowed, his mouth a firm angry line.

'Then why do you keep making me say it?' A little of her old spirit returned.

Dominic raised his eyebrows. 'I'm not making you say it.'

'Yes, you are. What's the matter with you, with *us*? You've been downright rude to me since we left the hospital yesterday.' She knew she wasn't getting through to him by the withdrawn expression on his face, if anything his eyes more glacial.

'I had work to do—I asked Charles to tell you.'

'And he did as you instructed. But I thought we'd gone past the stage where I had to be informed of your movements by a servant. Gail even had to tell me you were going away tomorrow—*you* didn't tell me.'

Dominic's mouth turned back. 'I don't remember being given the chance. You attacked me with it as soon as you came into the room.'

She flushed. 'I——'

'For God's sake don't say you're sorry again!' he snapped.

Her eyes flashed angrily. 'I wasn't about to, I have nothing to apologise for. You don't want me any more, is that it?' She came straight to the point.

His grey eyes slid over her almost insolently. 'Oh, I still want you. You're very desirable, especially when you're angry.'

'But that's it, isn't it? That's as far as your feelings for me go. You can't feel love for any woman, only desire. And desiring me is a little too complicated for you to want to get involved in,' she accused. 'It's all right to have your women up in London, but I'm a little too close to home, almost a member of your family. With me things can't be quite as simple and unemotional, other people get drawn into it.'

'Have you quite finished?'

'No, I haven't! I told you yesterday that you're afraid of life, I still think that.'

'You're entitled to your opinion.' He walked over to the door. 'Excuse me.'

'Dominic!'

'Yes?' he asked uncompromisingly.

'Dominic, don't go,' Alexandra pleaded.

'I have some work to get through, telephone calls to make.'

'I didn't mean now. Don't go to London tomorrow. Stay here with me,' she begged.

'I explained my reasons for leaving to Gail.'

She ran to his side, her hand on his arm beseechingly. 'Then explain them to me, Dominic. Explain them to me!'

He put her savagely away from him. 'I don't have to explain anything to you. You don't own me. No woman does that.'

'But I—I thought I meant something to you.' Her voice broke as she struggled to hold back the tears. 'I thought we meant something to each other.'

'Because of a few kisses and a few words of love?' he scorned. 'How naïve you are, Alexandra! Your friend Young was right, your innocence soon begins to pall. I'm going back to London because I want a real woman in my arms, a woman I can make love to and not have to feel guilty about it.'

'Sabrina Gilbert,' she whispered brokenly.

'Yes. I thought I could take you with promises of marriage, and forget about you as easily, but I find I can't do that to you or to Gail and Trevor. You're right when you say you're too close to home. I should have known better than to get involved with you,' he added cruelly.

'But I never asked for marriage. I've never tried to stop you making love to me.'

'No,' he agreed sneeringly. 'But the places you chose weren't exactly suitable for what I had in mind.'

'I don't believe that's it,' she denied. 'It's something else, something that happened yesterday afternoon. You were talking to me of marriage yesterday!' she reminded him desperately.

He shrugged. 'Only because I wanted you. But like I said, it all involves Gail and Trevor, and I can do without that hassle.'

'But you love me! I know you do. I'll show you.' Alexandra stood on tiptoe to kiss him, her arms about his neck, her mouth moving with a fierce desperation on his.

For a moment he seemed to weaken, his mouth responding, then he pushed her away from him, ripping her arms from about his neck. 'I've never mentioned love to you—or any other woman for that matter!'

'No, but you——'

'I don't love you, Alexandra,' he bit out curtly. 'You've read far too much into what could only ever have been a flirtation on my part, a brief affair at most.'

'But you said we'd get married in six months!'

'Six months is a long time,' he said with a cruel smile. 'Quite long enough for me to have got out of it. I once told you that it would be your love that would break me, and it's certainly done that. You should think yourself lucky, it's only guilty conscience on my part that's stopped me taking you—you certainly haven't tried to stop me.'

Alexandra swallowed hard, a terrible sickness rising

up in her throat. 'I think I hate you now.'

'Perhaps that's as well.'

She turned away. 'I hate you!'

Dominic hesitated in the open doorway, his gaze resting on her bent head. 'Are you all right?'

'Yes,' she mumbled.

'I—I'll call you from London if you like,' he suggested softly.

Her head shot up, anger in her eyes. 'Don't bother! I don't need your sympathy. I'll get over this infatuation I have for you, all the easier because I now know it was all a game to you.'

'Not a game, Alex. I——'

'Don't call me that!' She brushed past him. 'You can keep your seduction routine for those who appreciate it. I find it just sickens me!'

In fact she did only just reach the bathroom before she was violently sick. Dominic had been playing with her all the time, her love meant nothing to him. She cried herself to sleep that night, deep choking sobs that made her body ache.

When she came downstairs the next morning it was to find that Dominic had already left. She had wanted to see him before he left, to find out if he truly meant the things he had said, his absence seemed to make that unnecessary.

During the next few days she lived in nervous anticipation of him calling her as he had said he would, had hoped he would telephone even though she had told him not to. But he didn't, and her misery grew. She had even wondered if perhaps he would return on Friday as he usually did, but by midnight she knew he wasn't going to.

She hesitated about telephoning his apartment all the next day, knowing she ought to have more pride. But she couldn't go on like this, living in his house, sur-

rounded by memories of him wherever she went, by the
faint aroma of the cheroots he often smoked. She had
to speak to him, even if she lost all her pride by doing
so.

The telephone rang for a long time before it was
picked up, a man answering, but certainly not Dominic.
She could hear the sound of loud music, laughter, and
people shouting, noise so loud that she had to shout
above it to make herself audible to the man.

He finally seemed to understand her, or at least she
thought he had, until five minutes later when no one
came back to answer the telephone. There was obviously a party going on there, and the man had sounded
slightly tipsy.

Finally she heard the receiver being picked up again
and a female voice came down the line this time. 'Can I
help you in any way?' she asked huskily.

Alexandra explained for the second time in a matter
of minutes that she wanted to talk to Dominic.

'Dominic!' she heard the woman shout. 'Dominic,
there's a call for you. Darling?' she said in a husky
drawl.

Alexandra froze as she recognised that voice, the
way the woman called Dominic, 'darling'. She slowly
replaced the receiver. So Dominic had meant it when
he said he was going back to Sabrina Gilbert, because
that was surely who had been on the other end of the
telephone.

CHAPTER TEN

THINKING rationally about the things Dominic had said to her, Alexandra knew he had been lying about the fact that she was to be just another affair to him, knew it because there were too many occasions when she had shamelessly offered herself to him and he had fought for the control not to take her.

He *had* been serious about marrying her in six months' time, but something had happened to change his mind. He had deliberately hurt her, said cruel things to her. But even so that didn't alter the fact that he had gone straight back to Sabrina Gilbert!

It was because of this that her emotions felt numb as far as Dominic was concerned. She didn't hate him as she had told him she did, but she certainly didn't love him any more either, she just felt nothing for him at all. The part of her heart that had belonged to him was now a black void.

She was neither happy or sad, the loving time with Dominic seeming not to have happened. What had it really been after all—two or three days when they had deluded themselves there could be more than antagonism between them.

She stayed on at his house, only moving back home when Gail at last came out of hospital, the baby now a big part of their family. Everyone seemed to revolve their life about him now, and charming little monkey that he was, he revelled in every moment.

Alexandra tickled him under the chin. 'I think he's going to be like his uncle after all.' She laughed as he blew bubbles at her. 'You'll have all the girls falling for you when you're older, young man!' She picked him up and kissed him.

Gail lay on the sofa, still a little bruised from her operation but otherwise very happy. She put the last 'thank-you' letter in her neat little pile, glad that task was over. It was lovely of people to send her gifts for the baby, but she hated all the letter writing afterwards.

She looked closely at Alexandra. 'Are you over Dominic now?' she asked gently.

Alexandra's expression didn't alter. 'There wasn't a lot to get over.' She held her nephew firmly in her arms, smoothing back his fluffy hair.

'He's been to see me a couple of times, you know.'

Alexandra frowned, studiously straightening her nephew's little suit. 'No, I didn't know.'

'He asked me not to tell you,' Gail admitted.

Alexandra gave a hard laugh. 'Whatever did he do that for? Did he imagine I'd rush down to the hospital and make a scene?' she scorned. 'He could have saved himself the trouble of sneaking about, I'm not that interested in what he does.'

'Don't be too hard on him, Alexandra. To tell you the truth he looks terrible, much worse than he did after his time in Africa. He looks ill, he's so pale and drawn.'

'It's all that high living,' Alexandra said callously. 'Come on, monkey, let's go and post Mummy's letters.' She settled the baby in his pram. 'The fresh air will put some colour in his cheeks.'

'About Dominic,' Gail persisted. 'He——'

Alexandra gave a bright smile. 'I really don't want to know anything about him.' She picked up the letters Gail had so laboriously written. 'Is this all of them?'

'Yes. But about Dominic——'

'I'm not interested, Gail,' she repeated firmly. 'I'm taking the baby for a walk to post these letters. We'll all sit out in the garden afterwards, shall we?'

Gail sighed. 'Yes, okay. But I wish you'd listen to me about——'

'Well, I won't. See you later,' she called gaily.

It was a beautiful day outside, the sun shining brightly, the birds singing in the trees. A truly lovely day.

Alexandra chattered all the way down the road to her sleepy nephew, until she reached the local shop that also contained the post office, when she realised he had fallen asleep.

The door to the shop stood open and after checking that the baby would be all right for a few minutes she went inside. Mrs Saunders was dealing with another customer at the back of the shop when she went in and so she flicked idly through the selection of birthday cards.

'She stayed at his house all those weeks, you know,' she heard Mrs Saunders twitter, a small bird-like woman who moved in quick nervous movements but never actually seemed to get anything done. 'Disgusting, I call it.'

'Why's that?' The customer hadn't heard this snippet of gossip.

Alexandra smiled at their busybodying, wondering whose fate it was to be ripped to shreds by their malicious tongues today.

'Well,' Mrs Saunders was obviously warming to the subject now, 'It's all over the village about the way they've been carrying on together.'

'I haven't heard anything,' the other woman replied.

'No—well, you were away on holiday when it all came out into the open. She isn't going to marry the Young boy now, of course.'

Alexandra froze. This wasn't just the innocent actions of one of the village women being misconstrued, this was *her*! She was so shocked she couldn't move.

'Mrs Young wouldn't allow it,' the customer replied.

'Not if what you say about her and Dominic Tempest is true.'

'Oh, it's true all right.' Her voice lowered. 'Apparently Roger Young saw them out together at a restaurant twenty miles from here. Trying to hide their affair, no doubt, not expecting anyone from about here to see them.'

'Ooh, how terrible!' the other woman exclaimed with relish, obviously thinking no such thing. 'And you say it's been going on some months now?'

'*I* don't say it, the Youngs do. Of course they could just be saying it because their son has been made to look a little foolish. But Alexandra's always been a bit wild, going her own way regardless of conventions.'

'Dominic Tempest must have encouraged her,' the customer said knowingly. 'You know what these show-business types are like.'

'He's been back in London several weeks now,' Mrs Saunders told her. 'Obviously just a ploy to allay suspicion from them both. They're probably meeting somewhere else at the moment. Much too blatant to stay in that house together.'

Alexandra had heard enough, wanting only to escape before she was sick. She stumbled out of the shop, still undetected by the two gossiping women. Oh God, how could those people think such things of her, how could they!

She walked quickly back to the house, moving automatically, the tears streaming down her cheeks and blurring her vision. But another shock awaited her when she got back—Dominic's Ferrari parked in the driveway. She quickly wiped the tears away, determined not to let anyone see how upset she had been. What had it been after all, merely the distorted gossip of a couple of malicious women who had nothing better to do with their time. But that didn't make it hurt any less!

Right now she had to go into the house and face Dominic, their first meeting since he had told her it had all been a game to him. She picked up the baby, careful not to wake him, and left the pram outside.

Gail and Dominic were in the lounge, Dominic surrounded by a haze of cheroot smoke as usual, although she agreed with her sister, he did look tired and ill. Still, that was nothing to do with her. If he wanted to kill himself with women and work that was up to him.

He was watching her now, the expression in his eyes unreadable as she turned away to put her sleeping nephew in his cot. Dominic had no right to look at her like that, not when he had discarded her love so easily.

'All right?' Gail asked softly.

She smiled brightly. 'Yes, fine.'

'Did you post the letters?'

The smile faded from her face and she pulled the letters out of the back pocket of her denims. She had forgotten all about them in her haste to get away. 'I—I forgot,' she said lamely.

Gail looked puzzled. 'But that's why you went out.'

'Yes. Well, I—I——' Alexandra looked desperately from Gail to Dominic, aware only that he was giving her an odd look. 'I just forgot.' She ran to the door, tears welling up in her eyes again. 'Excuse me,' she cried chokingly before she fled.

Dominic being here after all the things she had just heard was all too much for her, and she flung herself down on to the bed, sobbing brokenly. He shouldn't be here, he had no right, no right. He should have stayed with his friends in London, not come back here to add fuel to the gossip—even if it was unfounded.

She felt the bed give beside her and turned to throw herself into Gail's arms. But it wasn't Gail, this body was definitely male, and the arms were familiar to her. She was in Dominic's arms! She tried to pull away from him, but he held her firm.

'Alex,' he shook her gently. 'Alex, look at me!'

She did so, her eyes purple smudges of pain. 'Hello, Dominic,' she said dully.

'Hello,' he returned huskily, looking at her with concern. 'Now, tell me what the tears are for?'

She drew a ragged breath. 'It—it isn't important.'

'Important enough to make you cry,' he insisted. 'And it wasn't simply that you forgot to post a few unimportant letters.'

She pushed back her tangled black hair. 'You shouldn't be up here.' She moved out of his arms and went over to the mirror, smoothing away the tears, but the evidence of their having been there was in her reddened cheeks and wet lashes. 'People will talk,' she muttered bitterly.

Dominic frowned, still sitting on the rumpled bed. 'What people? There's only Gail downstairs.'

'People have a way of finding out these things.'

'I don't see how—' He looked at her sharply. 'Did someone say something to you? Is that why you're upset?'

Alexandra shook her head. 'No one said anything to me,' she told him truthfully.

He stood up, dwarfing her bedroom, his body leaner than she remembered in the fitted black silk shirt and black corduroys. 'You have to tell me why you were upset, Alex. I have to know.'

His manner aroused the anger in her. 'I don't *have* to tell you anything, Dominic. If I want to cry then I'll damn well cry. I don't have to explain my reasons to you.'

'I came here today to speak to you.'

She gave him a sharp look. 'Why should you want to speak to me?' she asked coldly. 'I thought we'd said all there was to say weeks ago.'

'I telephoned Trevor yesterday and asked him if he would give me his permission to marry you,' he told her quietly.

'You did *what*?' she burst out, staring at him in disbelief.

'I want to marry you,' he repeated.

'Really?' she said shrilly. 'Didn't it occur to you to ask me before you approached Trevor?'

'I had already asked you weeks ago. I thought you——'

'Well, you had no right to *think* anything as far as I'm concerned,' she interrupted harshly. 'I don't want to marry you.'

He paled even more, his skin sallow. 'Three weeks ago you——'

'I was told by you that I meant nothing more to you than a brief affair at most.'

'I love you, Alex.'

If Dominic had told her this a few weeks ago she would have been overjoyed, but it had come too late, too late to stop the cold hard shell that now encased her heart for him. 'What am I supposed to say to that?' she enquired coolly.

'That you love me too?' he said hopefully.

'But I don't,' she told him callously. 'Not any more.'

Dominic took a step towards her. 'But you can't have just changed your mind.'

'Why not? You have.'

'But I *love* you,' he said forcefully. 'I love you, Alex!'

She nodded. 'And I suppose I should feel flattered by that, when you could just walk out on me, could just cruelly tell me that you want me but don't want the trouble involved in going out with me. You say you love me—how long for? Until you have what you want and can change your mind again? Forget it, Dominic. You taught me a harsh lesson, but I *did* learn it.'

He pulled her into his arms, kissing her with fierce desperation. 'I love you, Alex,' he said raggedly. 'Please don't turn me away,' he pleaded, his mouth gentle on hers now, cajoling rather than demanding. 'Kiss me, Alex,' he begged as he gained no response from her.

She felt cold, his lips on hers pleasant but no more than that. 'I have no wish to kiss you.'

His look was agonised, but his arms tightened about her. 'I'll make you want me. I have to make you want me,' he said grimly. 'I've been going through hell since I went to London, wondering what you were doing, who you were with.'

'You left of your own free choice.'

'No, no, I didn't. I left because I knew I loved you, and it scared the hell out of me.'

Alexandra turned away. 'You aren't making much sense. You say you left because you loved me, and yet before you went you told me the opposite.'

'Yes,' he sighed. 'That night the baby was born I knew beyond doubt that I loved you, knew that if I ever had to go through that with you I wouldn't be able to stand it. And so I did what you accused me of, I ran away. I ran away from life and committing myself to one person.'

And went back to Sabrina Gilbert and woman like her! That was the one thing she would never be able to forget, even if she forgave him for everything else. 'And now you've changed your mind.'

'Yes! Because I found I can't live without you. I would rather have the pain of being completely vulnerable where you're concerned than go through the agony of being without you. I want to marry you, make you mine for all time. I telephoned Trevor and asked him because I want to marry you now, not in six months' time, but now.'

'And what did he say?'

'He told me to come down today and ask you myself.'

So that was what Gail had been trying to tell her before she went out. 'And I'm saying no,' she said calmly.

'But why? You said this was what you wanted.'

'Not any more. It's gone, Dominic, the feeling has all gone. You killed it that night you ridiculed the way I felt.'

'Because I hurt you,' he acknowledged. 'Of course I did. But I can kiss the hurt away, get through the pain I caused by my brutality. Will you let me try?'

She shrugged. He could kiss away the pain, but he couldn't alter the fact that he had been with other women during his absence, certainly with Sabrina Gilbert if no other woman. 'You can try,' she told him. 'But I don't think it will work.'

'It *has* to.' He bent his head, parting her lips with his, his arms straining her to him as his mouth begged for her response.

Alexandra made no effort to resist him, feeling the usual pleasure and desire she felt when in his arms, but knowing none of the flood of love she usually felt when this close to him. It was as if she were standing apart from him, watching with casual interest the expertise he used to try and arouse her.

He lowered her gently on to the bed, parting her tee-shirt from her denims to caress the smooth flesh beneath. Alexandra liked his hands on her body, but that was all; other than that she felt numb and far removed from him.

Dominic looked up at her. 'This means nothing to you, does it?'

She smiled. 'Well, you haven't lost your expertise, if that's what you mean.' How could he when he had been keeping in practice with the lovely Sabrina Gilbert! 'You can still make me want you.'

'But that's all?'

'That's all.'

'You don't love me,' he said with finality, his hands dropping away from her as he slumped back on the bed at her side.

Alexandra stood up, straightening her hair with cool detachment. 'I already told you I didn't.' She tucked her tee-shirt back into her denims.

Dominic took his arm from over his eyes. 'I do love you, Alex,' he said softly.

'And I believe you. I'm even flattered, but it came too late. A few weeks earlier and I would probably have been your slave for life, grateful for whatever love you cared to give me.' Might even have been stupid enough to ignore his affairs! 'But not now. I seem to have found that maturity you always said I lacked. By the way, some of that gossip you said would be flourishing about us still seems to be going the rounds. In fact the people in the village think we've been having assignations while you've been in London, conveniently far away from here, of course.'

'So that's what upset you today,' he guessed. 'What else did they have to say?'

'Oh, not a lot,' she dismissed. 'I was just being silly earlier, allowing them to get under my skin.'

He stood up, looking down at her, smoothing the hair back tenderly from her face. 'If I've done this to you, I'm sorry,' he said gently.

She met the love clearly visible in his eyes with indifference. 'Done what to me?'

'Made you hard and uncaring.'

She laughed, moving away from him. 'Rather like you in the past.'

Dominic drew a ragged breath. 'Yes, exactly like me in the past. Is that why you're doing it, to punish me? Because if you are it's working. I feel hellish.'

'You flatter yourself if you think I would bother with such things. I'm acting like I am because I feel nothing for you, nothing for you at all.'

His shoulders slumped. 'That's that, then.'

'Yes.'

'I'll go.' But still he hesitated.

'Yes.'

Gail was alone except for the baby when Alexandra came downstairs five minutes later. 'Dominic's just left,' she told her.

Alexandra nodded, sitting down on the sofa. 'I heard the car.'

'He's pretty broken up,' Gail continued. 'He's trying not to show it, but I know him too well. I've never seen him like that before, uncertain of himself, no self-confidence.'

'He'll get over it.'

Gail shook her head. 'No, he won't. He loves you, Alexandra. I never thought I would see the day he fell like us other mortals, but I've seen it today.'

'He doesn't love me, Gail—at least, not as I know love. It means something different to me.'

'He does love you,' her sister insisted. 'I admit I was a little sceptical about it when he spoke to Trevor yesterday. I didn't believe it at first, but I do now.'

'What did Trevor have to say about it?' Curiosity was getting the better of her now.

'What could he say? Besides, he thought it was up to you what you wanted to do. He never did like having to interfere between you and Roger.'

'But he turned out to be right about that.'

'Yes,' Gail agreed. 'And he's right about this too. He believes you to be in love with Dominic. And I'm sure of it.'

'No!' Alexandra denied vehemently. 'Dominic doesn't know the meaning of love.'

'Why do you think that? Surely there's only one way to be in love.'

'He's still seeing Sabrina Gilbert!' she burst out. 'Perhaps you don't know about her, Gail, but he's been having an affair with her for months.' She stood up to pace the room. 'She was there the day I went over to his house to tell him what I thought of him for interfering in my life, she met him at the airport when he came back from Africa, and last of all,' she took a deep breath, 'she was at his flat when I called him a couple of weeks ago.'

'After his return to London?'

'Yes.'

'And that's why you've built up this wall against him?'

'Shouldn't I have done?' Alexandra demanded. 'He said he knew he loved me when he left for London. If he can have her now he could have her after we were married.'

'Tell me about this Sabrina Gilbert being at his flat.'

Alexandra did so, explaining all about the noisy part she had heard going on in the background. 'It really sounded as if he were missing me,' she added dryly.

'Just because this woman was at his apartment it doesn't mean she was there with him.'

'She called him darling.'

'So what? It's a common affectation amongst actresses. There was a party going on, Alexandra, as a friend of his she was bound to be there.'

Alexandra remembered the way Dominic had said he couldn't bring himself to make love to the actress. 'Do you really think that's the way it was?' Uncertainty entered her voice.

'I think you ought to give him the chance to explain.'

'But I—— No! No, I still maintain he doesn't know how to love. He hurt me dreadfully.'

'He's resigned from his job.' Gail watched her closely

to gauge her reaction.

Alexandra looked shattered. 'He's *what*?'

'Resigned,' Gail repeated calmly. 'He wants to marry you and he doesn't think he should carry on with that job, not knowing the danger involved.'

'I—I don't understand—' Alexandra crumpled, the barrier she had put up against Dominic slowly evaporating. 'He's done this for *me*?'

'Yes,' Gail confirmed.

'Oh, God,' she choked. 'And I sent him away! I was awful to him, Gail, really awful!'

Gail squeezed her hand. 'It isn't too late. Go to him now.'

'After what I said to him I don't think he would want to see me.'

'The state he was in when he left here I think he would see you any time, day or night. Go and put him out of his misery.' Gail halted Alexandra at the door. 'I'll—er—I'll see you when I see you.'

Alexandra gave a glowing smile. 'Yes.'

When she reached the house she felt as if she had played this scene before—letting herself quietly into the house, Dominic slumped in a chair, the empty glass dangling from his hand, the look of abject misery on his face.

But this time he didn't scowl when he saw her, rising slowly to his feet, his grey eyes avidly searching her face. 'Alex!' he breathed her name softly.

'Just tell me if you were seeing Sabrina Gilbert when you were in London the last few weeks.' She came straight to the point, his answer to his question vitally important to her.

He looked surprised by the question, even mystified. 'I've seen her, yes, but not in the way you mean.'

'I had to know because I telephoned you and she answered. There was a party going on, by the noise I could hear.'

'There seem to have been a lot of parties lately,' he said grimly. 'But I think I know the one you mean—I remember answering the telephone only to find it was dead.'

'I rang off,' she explained.

'You thought I was with Sabrina?'

'Yes.'

'After what I'd told you about the last time I'd seen her?'

'The only thing that seemed important at the time was that she was there,' she said stubbornly.

He nodded. 'She was there, with some producer or other. I haven't been with other women, Alex. I tried, I won't deny it, but no one attracted me. It isn't easy admitting to yourself that you've fallen in love for the first time in your life at thirty-four, especially when it happens to be a mere child that you love. This last few weeks I've been trying to convince myself that I was mistaken. I finally gave up and admitted defeat.'

'And I turned you down,' she said softly.

'Yes,' he agreed dully.

'Gail said you've resigned from your job,' she continued.

Dominic turned away to replenish his glass with whisky. 'That's right,' he nodded.

'Why?'

'I'm sure she told you that too.'

'She did, but I would like to hear it from you.'

His eyes narrowed. 'Why, so that you can have something else to gloat over?' He angrily ignored the way she flinched, slamming his glass down on the table and moving forward to shake her roughly. 'I suppose you think I owe you this at least.' He pushed her roughly away from him. 'All right, Alex, I suppose I do owe you something. When Trevor was going through the agony of not knowing whether Gail was going to live or die I discovered I loved you, but I also discovered something else. I realised for the first time exactly what you must have gone through when I was in Africa, and I decided I had no right to put you through that again.'

Alexandra frowned. 'But you love your job.'

'I love you more.'

Now she knew it was true, knew that she was the most important thing in his life. He hadn't been prepared to make this sacrifice for any other woman, not his first wife or any woman since. Any final barrier she might have had against him crumpled into the dust and she could only see the pain and disappointment on his face, emotions she had caused by her cold cruelty.

'Oh, Dominic,' there were tears in her eyes now. 'I'm sorry, so sorry!'

He shrugged. 'You can't help the way you feel. I'll return to London immediately and save you any embarrassment my presence here could cause you.'

'You most certainly will not,' she denied, realising he had misunderstood the reason for her apology.

He looked at her uncertainly. 'I won't?'

'No,' she smiled at him, a smile full of her love for him. 'You can stay here and help me arrange the wedding.'

'Ours?' he asked hopefully.

'Oh, definitely.' She still smiled, moving into his arms to raise her face invitingly. 'I love you, Dominic. I love you very much.'

His hands trembled as he touched her face, searching her features as if unsure of her sincerity. 'But you said——'

She silenced him by placing her fingertips over his lips, shivering with delight as she felt him kissing her sensitive skin. 'I was hurt, darling, hurt and bewildered. For a while I really thought I did hate you, but that was only because I loved you so much. I know how silly that sounds, but it's the truth. Gail brought me to my senses after you'd left.'

'Clever Gail,' he said huskily. 'Can I kiss you now?'

'Yes, please,' she answered shyly.

'You'll respond this time? I don't think I could bear your coldness towards me again.'

'Try me,' she invited.

His mouth touched hers, tenatively at first, deepening the kiss as her mouth flowered beneath his, his arms straining her to the hardness of his body. His touch soon had her trembling and aroused within seconds, their bodies heated and on fire for each other.

Dominic buried his face in her throat and she wasn't sure if the tears on her cheeks were from her own happiness or his. He held her to him as if he would never let her go again—and she hoped he never would.

'You don't have to give up your job for me, Dominic.' He would never know the effort it cost her to say this. 'It's part of your life, a part you enjoy.'

He shook his head. 'Not any more, not if it takes me away from you. And we—we could have a family one day.'

'We could?' she asked breathlessly.

'Yes,' he said huskily.

'Oh, Dominic, I love you!'

He smiled tightly. 'I've been offered the chance of directing and appearing in another current affairs programme that will keep me closer to home. Any overseas work will be carried out by someone else.'

'And will you like that?' Alexandra realised that the subject of a family was still a touchy one as far as he was concerned, but at least he had talked about it.

'Any new show is a challenge, and I like challenge. Look how long it's taken me to tame you,' he added teasingly.

She quirked an eyebrow. 'You think I'm tamed?'

He laughed softly. 'I know you're not, but I like

your wildness, I always have. How long do you think it will be before we can be married?'

'A couple of months, I suppose.' She heard him groan. 'What's wrong?'

'I want you now.'

'I'm not saying no,' she told him throatily. 'And Gail more or less told me to stay here as long as I wanted to.'

'She's becoming very broadminded—but I'm not,' he said firmly. 'I have no intention of making love to you until we're married.'

'Back to the cold showers?' she teased.

Dominic grimaced. 'I guess so.'

'Poor darling!' she smoothed back his blond hair.

His arms tightened about her. 'But that doesn't mean I can't kiss you.'

She looked at him below lowered lashes. 'I hope not.'

'Although it will be up to you not to be too much of a temptation.'

Alexandra gave him a demure look. 'Yes, darling.'

He gave a triumphant laugh. 'I bet,' he chuckled. 'Never mind, I think this kind of hell I can take.' He bent to kiss her again.

Alexandra looked anxiously at her husband, knowing the last hours had been traumatic ones for him. Perhaps she had been selfish after all to have made him suffer the agony of seeing her go through childbirth, but to her the ultimate end had seemed worth it—the beautiful baby lying in the cot beside her bed, their daughter Emma.

The last eighteen months of marriage to Dominic had been the happiest time she had ever known, their love deepening and becoming more precious to each of them as each day passed. But her happiness had reached new heights when she had found she was to have Dominic's child. Dominic had seemed pleased too, but throughout her pregnancy she had known he had an overwhelming dread of the actual birth taking place.

And now it was over, and Dominic had stayed at her side through it all. He hadn't spoken a word since they had been left alone and she wasn't sure what to say to him. Had she made a terrible mistake in putting him through all this?—although it couldn't be said she was solely to blame. The physical side of their marriage had been perfect from their wedding night, and a family had really been inevitable, with the passion they had for each other.

She licked her lips. 'Dominic?'

He looked at her dazedly, dragging his gaze away from the sleeping baby. 'Mm?' he asked vaguely.

'Do you like her?'

'Like her?' he repeated.

'The baby,' she prompted.

He smiled, a deep tender smile that encompassed them both. 'She's beautiful, like her mother,' he squeezed her hand as it lay on the bed. 'I wouldn't have missed seeing her born for anything, it was the most fantastic thing I've ever seen in my life.'

Alexandra was still a little uncertain. 'Really? You aren't just saying that?'

'It was beautiful, Alex,' he reassured her. 'Nothing like I expected it to be after Trevor's experience with Gail. And you were so good, my darling, I was so proud of you. I have only one complaint to make to my young daughter.'

'What's that?'

'She's made it impossible for me to make love to you just lately.'

She gave a husky laugh. 'Not for much longer!'

Dominic sat on the side of the bed, holding her fiercely against him. 'I hope not. I love you so much that the last few weeks have been a form of torture.'

'You surely didn't still find me attractive and desirable in that state?'

He kissed her gently on the mouth. 'I find you attractive and desirable all the time—even now,' and his mouth hardened with passion on hers.

Alexandra returned his kiss, the last shadow of uncertainty about having the baby at last removed. The baby had increased their love for each other, and that was the way it should be.

Best Seller Romances

Romances you have loved

Mills & Boon Best Seller Romances are the love stories that have proved particularly popular with our readers. They really are "back by popular demand." These are the other titles to look out for this month.

EDGE OF SPRING
by Helen Bianchin

After a brief and desperately disillusioning marriage, Karen had managed to keep all men at bay for five years. But she was having rather more trouble with Matt Lucas, who refused to take no for an answer. How could she convince him that she didn't want to have anything to do with him, ever?

BOOMERANG BRIDE
by Margaret Pargeter

Four years ago, when Vicki was expecting her husband Wade's child, he had thrown her out and told her never to come back. Yet now he was forcing her to return, with their son. Just what did he think he was doing? And why should Vicki obey him?

Mills & Boon
the rose of romance

Rebecca had set herself on course for loneliness and despair. It took a plane crash and a struggle to survive in the wilds of the Canadian Northwest Territories to make her change – and to let her fall in love with the only other survivor, handsome Guy McLaren.

Arctic Rose is her story – and you can read it from the 14th February for just £2.25.

The story continues with Rebecca's sister, Tamara, available soon.

SAY IT WITH ROMANCE

Accept 4 Best Selling Romances Absolutely FREE

Enjoy the very best of love, romance and intrigue brought to you by Mills & Boon. Every month Mills & Boon very carefully select 3 Romances that have been particularly popular in the past and re-issue them for the benefit of readers who may have missed them first time round. Become a subscriber and you can receive six superb novels every two months, and your personal membership card will entitle you to a whole range of special benefits too: a free newsletter, packed with exclusive book offers, recipes, competitions and your guide to the stars, plus there are other bargain offers and big cash savings.

**AND an Introductory FREE GIFT for YOU.
Turn over the page for details.**

As a special introduction we will send you
FOUR superb and exciting
Best Seller Romances – yours to keep Free
– when you complete and return
this coupon to us.

At the same time we will reserve a
subscription to Mills & Boon Bestseller
Romances for you. Every two months you
will receive the 6 specially selected
Bestseller novels delivered direct to your
door. Postage and packing is always
completely Free. There is no obligation or
commitment – you can cancel your
subscription at any time.

FREE BOOKS CERTIFICATE